End's Beginning

End's Beginning

A Novel of Past and Present

Sebastian Williams

iUniverse, Inc.
New York   Bloomington

End's Beginning
A Novel of Past and Present

iUniverse books may be ordered through booksellers or by contacting:

iUniverse
1663 Liberty Drive
Bloomington, IN 47403
www.iuniverse.com
1-800-Authors (1-800-288-4677)

ISBN: 978-1-4401-9687-4 (sc)
ISBN: 978-1-4401-9686-7 (dj)
ISBN: 978-1-4401-9688-1 (ebk)

Printed in the United States of America

iUniverse rev. date: 1/12/10

Preservation

Day One

High atop a mountainside path, five men had gathered in front of an entrance to a cavern. A scrawny, rough-looking man with grey-and-white hair was looking over the ridge toward the busy village they had come from with some annoyance as the small gathered pack were awaiting their last compatriot. The air was calm, and the skies were overly cloudy, causing shadows to cover all the land in view.

The scrawny man huffed. "Where is he?"

Dov stood and turned to his eldest brother, who was standing close to the mountain's jagged edge. "He is not running that late, Seff."

Seff rolled his eyes and turned away to face the entrance to the cavern, leaving his youngest brother, Dov, there to look over the precipice alone. Kabos was sitting on the ground near the end of the mountain path. He was scratching his potbelly.

"He is quite late, Dov. I am certain he has his reasons. You need not defend him when your only wish is to place those large hands on the prize sealed within this cavern."

Dov slowly took a few steps away from the cliff after shaking off his vertigo before turning to Kabos. "And you wish differently, Kabos? Remind me of who the merchant is among us?"

Kabos let out a small grin as he was fiddling with some miscellaneous items and materials found within his satchel to keep him busy. Gurion was pacing back and forth. He slammed his fist into the mountain's side.

Seff looked over and addressed his next of kin. "Be careful, Gurion. You could move a mountain with that strength of yours. We do not wish you to cause a landslide of rocks and block our entrance."

"Sorry." He tied back his long, russet-coloured hair, which seemed to encircle his head. "I was somewhat rash."

Standing in the background, Almon stroked his full beard with his left thumb and index finger while looking upwards toward the ever-darkening sky. "Looks like there will be rain."

Seff sneered. "What of it? We shall be warm and dry inside this cavern and not become soaked as those poor, unfortunate souls in town."

Kabos stopped fiddling with the items inside his satchel and looked up toward the sky. "That will not be true if we are to wait much longer on him."

Dov moved. He had a seat next to a boulder in the otherwise rock-free, circular space that extended from the mountain's path just off the cavern's entrance. He used it as one would use the back of a chair. "I truly do not mind the rain."

Almon was stroking his beard once more. "Still, one of us should invent something that we could hold in our hands to protect ourselves from the rain."

Kabos intriguingly looked over at Almon. "What did you have in mind?"

Seff interrupted the two with a somewhat sarcastic laugh. "Anything for a profit, right, Kabos?"

Kabos ignored Seff's comment and started talking business with Almon. As Kabos was coming up with some ideas for such a device, Gurion noticed something in the background as he was pacing inside the circle. He pointed out toward the distance. "Who is that in the background? Is that him?"

Seff's back was facing the distance. He did not glance over his shoulder to look. "It better be."

Dov stood up and walked over to Gurion. He spotted the figure Gurion mentioned coming up the mountainside. He was carrying a lit torch as he was steadily making his way up the mountain path to the rest of the small gathered tribe. Dov confirmed it was who they were waiting for. The rest turned and looked, except for Seff, who was still holding his position. Kabos took his right hand and ran it backwards over his bald head as he noticed the man was carrying what appeared to be some extra equipment.

"What else is there to bring?"

After a few moments, the man finally made his way up the mountainside to the rest of the assembled. He set down his extra satchels and backpacks on the ground.

"Glad to see you could finally make it here, Oren," Seff said, growling.

"I am not that late." With his left hand, he pointed to his bags on the ground. "I brought extra provisions in case some unforeseen circumstances occur."

Kabos looked down at the satchels and noticed there had to be more than just extra provisions held within them.

Before he could ask, Oren continued, "I also brought additional wooden rods and rags soaked in pitch in the event we burn our torches down to nothing or one of our lights die out."

"Never mind the lights and wood, Oren." Dov said. "What spare provisions did you bring?"

Even though no one could see his face, Seff rolled his eyes. "Always with the stomach, Dov."

Dov ignored Seff and listened to Oren's response. "Some bread, extra wine and water, fruit. The basics needed for survival."

"Would the extra fruit not rot quickly, Oren?" Dov asked.

"If properly cared for and preserved, it should last long enough."

Gurion and Dov looked at each other.

"It is a shame that it is not meat or fish." Gurion remarked. "But it is a good thing that you thought ahead, Oren."

Seff turned and scowled at his two younger brothers. "Stop thinking with your stomachs, and let us get underway."

Seff's eyes shifted to Oren. "You are sure that the map you found with the ancient prize sealed within belongs to this cave?"

Oren nodded his head. "Yes, I am sure of it."

"How did you come into possession of such a map?" Kabos asked.

Seff laughed. "Yes, Oren, how did you? When it comes to finding these types of items, I would have placed my money on Kabos finding it."

Kabos tried not to smirk at Seff's comment. Oren shook his head back and forth playfully before answering. "Do you three remember that traveling scholar who used to teach us all those years ago?"

Seff, Gurion, and Kabos looked at each other.

"You will have to be more specific, Oren," Kabos said.

"The one who always said I was built solid. He had reddish hair and a deep voice."

The three knew who Oren was talking about now.

"How has that eccentric tutor been?" Seff asked.

"He is fine, Seff. He was in town a few days ago. I met him on the road, and we went to dinner to catch up on events over the past eighteen years. We debated and talked as if no time had passed at all. Details aside, after the meal, he left, but the map fell out of one of his pockets as he rose. I picked it up and rushed out to give it back to him, but, by the time I realized and made my way outside, he was gone."

Gurion looked perplexed. "Gone?"

"It was almost as if he vanished." Oren said as he looked toward Gurion.

Kabos scratched the top of his bald head. "People do not simply vanish into thin air. You probably just lost him in the crowd."

"Granted," Oren reluctantly agreed. "Still, it almost seemed as if he wanted me to have it. You remember him and his ways."

Seff rolled his eyes. "That I do. I also remember how you were always his favourite student."

Oren wondered if Seff was right before scanning the assembled. He knew each of them for quite some time. Seff was the eldest of the three brothers. Despite his small, scrawny figure, he was straightforward and highly aggressive at times. His hazel eyes were made all the more prominent due to his massively scarred face. Gurion was the middle child of the three brothers. He was strong, muscular, and fierce with a full set of russet-coloured hair accompanied by blue eyes. Dov was the youngest of the three and the rest of the assembled. Covered in brown hair with dark brown eyes, he was the tallest of the six and usually walked hunched over. He was also strong, yet laid-back most of the time. Kabos was the short, bald, potbellied profiteer of the group with light brown eyes. He would sell his soul if he thought he could turn a profit. And finally, there was Almon, the newest member of the group at average size and weight with piercing grey eyes. He was very observant, and he had a full, chestnut-coloured beard.

"Does everyone have their weapons ready at their arm's reach? Who knows what ungodly types of creatures we may encounter inside this cavern?"

The five looked into Oren's dark brown eyes. They all agreed in some form or another as they clutched their crudely made swords. Almon decided to ask the question that was on everyone's mind. "It is still equal shares. Right, Oren?"

"Yes," Oren said as he looked toward Almon. "It is equal shares. Did it seem as if it could be done any other way?"

"No," he said in a determined voice. "I merely wished it stated for the record."

Almon turned his head to Kabos. "Did you hear that? Equal shares. No bartering allowed."

Kabos turned his head to Almon. "I heard Oren."

He looked back toward Oren. "What does the map say comes next?"

Oren showed the tattered map and pointed to the trail on it. "Unfortunately, this is as far as it goes. It leads to this cave and shows a chest somewhere in the middle of it. I assume the rest is up to us seeing how it does not show a path on how to get to it."

Seff turned and started making his way toward the cavern's entrance. "Leave it to that eccentric bastard to chase a map only half-complete."

"Are we so much different?"

Seff had no comment toward Almon. Oren felt some driblets of rain on his shoulder. "It is starting to rain. Let us light our torches and start our descent."

With their covenant made, Seff and Almon lifted their torches and lit them from Oren's. The six companions picked up their backpacks and satchels from the ground and began their journey into the cave.

Once inside the cave, Seff was in the front of the group, leading the way down the narrow, dimly lit, oval-shaped hallway that lay just off the entrance. Behind him was the greedy Kabos. Almon was third in line, and this allowed him the distance he wished for so he could make his own observations. Behind him was the ferocious Gurion, followed by the enormous Dov who was walking hunched over. Last in line was sturdy Oren, keeping watch over the rest of the group.

After a few minutes, the small tribe of six began to hear the loud crack of thunder. Turning their heads, they glanced back toward the entranceway.

"With all of those gathered clouds, we will have quite the storm if some thunder and lightning joins the downpour," stated Almon.

Some of the companions looked a little skittish.

"It is nothing to be concerned about. It is just a storm," Oren said with reassurance.

A bright flash illuminated the darkened cave. The sound of thunder that followed caused the very ground they were standing on to tremble. The severity of the sudden storm taking place outside caused Seff's and Almon's torches to fall out of their hands as everyone struggled to find a wall to keep their balance. The lit torches combined together to create a larger illumination stemming from the ground a few feet away from them. Despite this and even though Oren held his flame, the light was not bright enough for them to fully see one another.

"Is everyone all right?" Oren asked.

Before anyone could answer, they heard something they could not place, but it seemed as if it were coming from the direction of the entrance. The dim light emanating from Oren's torch shone on Seff's scarred face as he slowly made his way past him toward the entrance. Suddenly, the noise forcefully echoed within the dark cavern as the entrance above the cave fell in with boulders and sealed the startled adventurers inside. Even though he was a few feet from the rocky doorway, Seff instinctively jumped back in order to avoid this landslide. After regaining their balance from this new trembling ground, the covenant of six looked around their new, darker surrounding.

"What just happened?" Dov asked in a confused tone.

Seff ran forward into the darkness. "We are trapped," he said, panicking as he checked the new wall for any cracks or holes with his hands.

There were none. It was completely sealed. Nothing could enter or leave the cavern from the opposite side now.

"Is it sealed?" asked Kabos with a cry.

Gurion stepped up to the rock wall and attempted to move it with his strength. He tried pushing the new cave wall forwards, but he could not do it alone. "Dov, come help me push."

Dov stepped up next to him and tried to help with his added size and strength. It was to no avail. Gurion and Dov stopped their push as Seff was still searching the rock face.

"Do not worry, friends." Oren optimistically declared. "There must be another way out."

Almon picked up a torch near his feet. As he looked around their new prison, he made his observations and seemed to run something across the rocky wall. Gurion turned around and spoke ferociously. He pointed in front of him. "This is all your fault, Oren."

Oren remained calm. In a soothing voice, he asked, "My friends, did we not all agree to partake in this?"

Reluctantly, the others quickly calmed down.

"We shall find the prize. Then we shall find another way out. This is nothing to worry about. There cannot be only one entrance to this large cavern, right?"

The others reluctantly agreed with him.

Kabos spoke first. "What happens next?"

"We have no choice other than to persevere," Oren replied. He turned to Seff in the dim and eerie light of their new prison. He placed his hand on his shoulder to stop him from searching the blocked entrance. "Seff," he said in a strong and confident voice, "we cannot leave from here though, I am sure you can find another exit for us." Seff stopped his search as Oren continued. "Are you up for the task?" Seff snickered as he regained his wits and picked up the remaining torch from the ground. "That I am."

With the three torches back in their owners' hands, they took their places in line once again. Seff was back in the front with Kabos, Almon, Gurion, Dov, and Oren behind him. The small covenant continued to move forward, down into the darker depths of the cave.

"Seff, how far ahead can you see?" Almon asked.

Seff snapped at him. "I can see fine. What of it?"

Almon continued, "What is it you see?"

Seff answered while staring forward. "I see one long corridor with no change in colour. It is a mixture of blue, purple, and brown. It is the same height and constant. Now leave me alone so I can concentrate on the path as I find it."

Kabos rubbed his hands greedily together. "I cannot wait until we find this prize."

"You certainly are eager about this prize," started Almon. "What are you going to do with your share?"

Kabos tilted his head slightly to the right as he thought. "There are many possibilities. Perhaps I will buy low-priced artifacts and then sell them at a higher price. I could modify them with simple crafts to make them appear exquisite and original."

Kabos greedily rubbed his hands once more as he continued directly behind Seff.

"Gurion? How about you?" Almon asked next.

Before he could answer, Seff interrupted. "He should hire someone to cut that mane of his."

Gurion ignored his older brothers' sarcasm and answered Almon. "I think I would become an outdoorsman full time. The thrill is exhilarating. Being able to live off the land in a small cabin and farm out in the wilderness a few days from civilization while hunting wild beasts for my dinner. I would not have to worry about money to make a living. If things ever became too difficult, as a drought or some other setback, I could return to the city for preserves and even stay in an inn for a few nights."

Dov spoke up from behind Gurion. "That sounds like an idea, brother. Sounds similar to what I wanted to do, except my house would not be so deep in the wilderness. It would be on the river. You all know that I never tire of fish."

Seff rolled his eyes. "We know. We know. I am surprised that the two of you are not potbellied like Kabos over there with all that you eat."

Kabos touched his round stomach. "Hey!"

Dov spoke loudly so Seff would hear him, even though he did not realize there was no need due to the echo within the cavern. "All right,

Seff. Since you seem to have a comment on everyone else's plans, what is yours?"

"I would roam around the world without having to needlessly work."

"One would think you would have grown tired of roaming by now, brother."

"That was not roaming Gurion. That was work. I want adventure. It is a must. Besides, when I come into a new area, I would assert myself as the dominant one over the people. It is my turn now that I will not have to labour for them. Maybe some would even join me in my endeavours."

Almon, who was rather close to Seff, asked, "So what you are saying is that you wish to govern yourself over a pack of subservient people?"

"Do we not all wish that in some form, you inquisitive pest?"

"Want what?" Almon answered. "To be a shepherd over a flock or a wolf in their guise?"

"Are most shepherds not wolves as they cultivate the flock for their own needs? Sure, they say it is to protect the animals but it is nothing more then a way for them to justify themselves."

Almon took a second. "I never thought of it that way."

Without truly wanting to know, Seff proceeded to ask Almon, "What will you do with your share?"

"I would have to wait and see."

Seff rolled his eyes as Almon continued his response. "Perhaps I would pay off my debts so I can be welcomed back in my home village once more."

Kabos looked slightly over his shoulder. "How about you, Oren?"

"I think I would use the profits to provide for my aging family."

"How sentimental of you, Oren."

"Why thank you, Seff," he replied.

"Could you not hear the sarcasm in my voice? One may think that you were modeling yourself after God."

Almon spoke up. "Now why would Oren want to model himself after God? He's a smiter."

Gurion spoke from behind Almon, "Care to clarify for us?"

"He kicked us out of the garden, for starters. What does that say about him? Look but do not touch. There is something that makes plenty of sense. Placing the forbidden fruit tree in the middle of a garden where we would always see it? Considering how we are made in his image, did he not know that we are curious enough to taste it?"

"He did provide for us though, regardless of our personalities," Dov reluctantly said in defence of his eldest brother. "We just did not do what we were told. I think that is the irony Seff was aiming for."

Almon defended his position. "I know what Seff was aiming for Dov. I am stating the facts. They are nothing more then stories, fables to keep us in order while we are young."

Gurion came to the aid of his younger brother. "Well, I am not so sure about that being a whole imagined story, but that would have been so nice. Being able to graze around on lush meadows all day long." Gurion sighed at what was lost to him without having ever experienced it.

Seff seemingly mocked Gurion. "What is the point of that? No survival instinct. No adventure. Life would have been incredibly dull in that sanctuary. Everything was provided. How could we strive toward a goal? We would not have any. Those two did the best thing possible for us. We are better off out in the world and not locked away in that insipid garden."

Kabos agreed with Seff.

Dov chimed in with his two cents. "There is no true surprise in that, Kabos. What profit would there to be gained in a sanctuary? God forbid."

Kabos looked back over his shoulder. He noticed Dov due to his size. "Exactly my point. Take a moment to think about it Dov. Would you not become bored seeing the exact same type of scenery every single day until the end of time?"

Dov's eyes looked toward the rock-solid ground. "I do not know." His eyes levelled. "I think I would have found it very relaxing. I could sleep under a tree all day without a worry in my head."

A somewhat abrasive huff came from the front of the line. "Of course you would have found it relaxing, you lazy sloth."

"What is that supposed to mean?" Seff stopped in his tracks. He turned around and made his way past Kabos, Almon, and Gurion. "You heard me, you brutish oaf. You wish to live near a river so you could step out and have a meal without having to go far away from your house. Why do you not just make some porridge and hibernate?"

Dov stood up straight and loomed over the smaller, scrawnier Seff. "I hate porridge. You know that. And what of you, you cocky, little snake? Like you are any better? You would—"

Before Dov could finish his comment, Almon interrupted the dispute with a comment of his own. "I think that, if anyone here is a snake, it would not be Seff. We all know that it would be Kabos."

Kabos let out a small chuckle of admittance. Almon's interruption did nothing to further ease the tension between the two siblings. Dov was still staring Seff down as he was searching for the words to finish his insult. Seff did not relent.

"Not too quick on the comebacks, are we, Dov? So much strength and so little brain. It is not a total loss. There is always a place for another strong, hairy dimwit in the world to help plow fields and do other menial tasks."

Dov formed a fist with his right hand and threw it toward Seff. Seff gracefully jumped backwards, but his back hit something solid. He knew it couldn't have been the cavernous wall. He turned around and became a little startled when he noticed Gurion showing his teeth. Seff sneered and started to show his while he gripped the hilt of his blade, which hung off his left side. Almon was watching this. Kabos was trying to get him to place a bet on who would win the fight. Suddenly, Oren stepped in between the two.

"Calm down, you three," he said, looking at the brothers. Oren turned to Gurion. "We need your strength." He looked at Dov. "Yours as well." He turned to Seff. "And we need your sense of direction. You direct our path. We are walking blind without you. We all need each other in this endeavour. Infighting will get us nowhere fast. Remember, we also have to find another way out of here in addition to the prize found on the map. Tell me. Do all of you wish to die in this cave?"

Seff removed his hand from the hilt as Gurion withdrew his teeth.

"That is better," Oren said.

Seff hastily pushed by and continued forward. The other five looked at each other and formed the line once again.

Day Nine

Three of the six torches were lit. One in front of the group lay on the ground while one was in the back. Oren was holding the third as he was sitting in the middle of the assembly. Next to him laid Gurion. Fast asleep on his back, his snores were echoing within the cavern. Dov was next to him, staring aimlessly upwards at the blackened ceiling. Seff was in his usual spot, but his nose was to the ground. He was trying to see if he could pick up any signs that may help the group reach their destination. To Seff's right, Almon was standing, using the cavern's wall to help support him. Kabos was standing to the left of Seff, but he finally took a seat next to Oren.

Kabos wiped his right arm across his forehead. "How long have we been in here?"

"It would appear to be somewhere between eight and ten days," Almon answered.

Dov looked toward Almon. "How can you tell? We cannot see the sun."

Almon scratched his right knee as he explained his way of making the time. "You estimate that we sleep for six to eight hours every time we stop, right?"

Dov nodded in the somewhat lightened darkness. "Consider the time we left, and count the amount of times we have slept to get an approximation of how long we have been in this place."

Dov shook his head, trying to follow the conversation. "It is too late for sums and numbers, or perhaps it is too early?"

"You would not be able to figure it out anyway," Seff said.

Dov turned his head to his left. "Your path finding has not been much better."

Seff forcefully breathed out his nose. "I did not construct the arrangement of this cavern. We have been walking in a straight line for as long as Almon has approximately said. There have been no intersections or other routes. The only difference in this path has been in the winding. The path goes downwards and then turns right, then upwards and left, then back down and straight, and so on."

Kabos looked up and over toward Seff. "What are you saying?"

Seff kept his nose to the ground. "One might figure that the path would have interlocked with itself by now, seeing how it has been going, but it has not. It does not make any sense. I have no idea how far we have walked in these past days. The inclines leading up and down are not steep at all. They are so subtle and gradual that we could actually be underground. The entrance was in the middle of the mountain. Now that I think of it, there is no possible way we could still be above the ground we started."

Seff sneezed from the dust on the cavern floor. His face almost hit the floor due to the force caused by the sneeze. He wiped his face with his right arm before continuing. "The path has been far too linear. We would have come out on one of the mountain's sides by now. I think we may have entered some type of underground tunnel system."

"Perhaps you missed a side opening in the walls and we have been traveling in a circle."

"No, Dov," Almon said. "He has not." He took something out of his satchel.

"Before we entered, I took this small, sharp rock from outside. I have been using it to mark the walls with horizontal lines as we go along. We have not come across a marking I have recorded yet."

Dov looked down. "I hate this cave."

"Question my direction and then settle when Almon backs me. How pitiable of you. I would have figured you would be comfortable and warm inside this cavern. Or is it all the walking that is making you whine?"

Dov didn't respond. Kabos' head leaned over and rested on Oren's right shoulder. He had passed out. Oren began to rummage through his bags. Seff stopped his searching and laid there on his stomach. Even though Gurion was asleep, his belly let out a hungry roar. Dov turned to his left. "His stomach makes a good point, Oren."

"I think we all agree with your brother's stomach, but we should wait until we wake. It will help give us the energy we need to continue on."

Dov's head sunk toward the ground. Oren reached over Gurion and sympathetically patted his companion. "Just remember not to overindulge yourself on your rations, my friend. I know you are not used to eating only one small meal a day, but you are doing well."

Dov was expecting to hear a comment from Seff, but he had fallen asleep. Almon let his back go and slid down the wall until he was sitting. Dov closed his eyes and quickly fell asleep. Almon followed suit. Oren looked around and noticed he was the only one still awake. He went about his bags once more, double-checking the emergency rations he had brought. He let out a tiny sigh and thought to himself that he should have brought more as it seemed the covenant of six would be in need of it soon. The preserves were still in good condition, but he knew they would only be able to last another seven days, ten tops, with the dank environment they were in. He brought his hands out of his bag and put down his torch. He took in a breath of stale air and closed his eyes.

Day Ten

The six woke up within moments of each other. Gurion leapt over Dov, who was staring up at the ceiling once again and ran past the still-burning torch that lay on the outskirts of the clan. Kabos stood up and outstretched his arms toward the cavernous sky while yawning. Almon sat there for a while after he opened his eyes. Seff scratched at his sides. Dov sat up and rubbed his eyes before he started going through his backpack in search of food. When Oren awoke, he stood up straight right away. The group heard Gurion spit, followed by the faint sound of his hands rubbing together.

He made his way back to the group and grumbled, "This has to be the worst part of living in a cave, having to relieve yourself in this way."

Kabos made his way past the oncoming Gurion and then past the still flame of the torch. Dov found some berries in his pack and started to devour them. Almon took some grapes out of his satchel. Gurion decided to have a drink of wine instead of eating anything, as the wine was starting to turn. He did not want it to go to waste. Seff removed the lid to a container of preserves and began eating some olives. After Kabos came back from relieving himself, he tried to bargain with Seff for his jar of olives with his single pomegranate. Oren was preoccupied with breaking off a piece of bread from the loaf he had in his satchel.

Kabos spoke to the group. "Remember that meal we had after our first sleep?"

"How could I not?" Dov's eyes lit up. "Cooked fish and steak over an open torch. Good thing we had our swords to hold the meat in place."

Seff and Gurion looked at each other, both remembering the taste of the steak they had eight days prior. Kabos let out a small drool at the thought of cooked meat.

Almon was putting his grapes back into his satchel, and he sighed. "It is too bad that the meat would not have stayed long in a cavern such as this. Some bird would be most appetizing right now."

Seff finished chewing an olive. "This is a cave, right? There are most likely bats, rats, or another form of living creature that reside in here. Keep an open eye for droppings or anything of the sort. If we find some, we can kill the creature that made them and cook it."

Gurion's stomach rumbled. "That would be a meal I think we could all go for, brother, except for Oren here, who only eats bread and fruit."

Almon spoke in defence of Oren. "Do not doubt Oren here, Gurion. He is the only one of us who was smart enough to bring many preserves instead of filling his bag full of flesh."

"Thank you for the praises, Almon," Oren said, "but you are giving me more credit than I am due."

Both Gurion and Kabos turned their heads toward Almon. "That is right. Almon does not know."

Almon looked at them. "What do I not know?"

"Oren has never eaten flesh," Gurion said. "As long as we have known him, it has been bread, soup, and fruit or vegetables."

Almon stroked his beard. "That is interesting."

"I cannot stomach it for some reason," Oren explained. "I have had it in the past, but the taste never took. Perhaps it was because it was something I did not need."

Seff finished his meal first and returned the jar of olives to his backpack. While the others were finishing, he picked up his burning torch and walked past the group to scout ahead. As he did this, the light around the group darkened. Oren grabbed his unlit torch after he finished eating his bread and made his way to the still-burning torch found on the outskirts. He picked it up and then returned to the group. He passed the unlit torch to Gurion and lit it. Dov stood up and lit his torch from Gurion's. Kabos and Almon left their torches unlit to conserve them. With a mutual understanding, they placed their preserves away and started to make their way forward. When they saw Seff in the distance, they noticed he was standing there very still and very silently. Because they were behind him, they could not see the look of disbelief on his face. They called to him, but he did not answer back.

Oren placed his right hand on Seff's shoulder once he reached him. "What is it?"

Kabos' tone became somewhat pushy as he called to the front. "Why did you stop?"

Seff shook his head to release his daze and threw his torch forward. It hit the ground, resonating within and illuminating the cavern just a little more. The others looked on and noticed that the cavern had widened. The six walked forward and stood side by side in the large area. From left to right stood Oren, Kabos, Seff, Gurion, Dov, and Almon. As the rejoined companions looked ahead of themselves, they noticed what Seff already knew. Three separate paths lay before them.

Gurion looked to his immediate left. "What do you make of this, Seff?"

He shook his head from side to side. "I have absolutely no idea."

Oren looked at the three entrances. Taking a few minutes, he pondered a few outcomes before offering a suggestion. "We have a few options."

The other five looked toward him.

"We could all go down one path together, or we could split into three groups of two and see where each separate route will take us. If we decide to separate, we will be more vulnerable, but we will be able to cover more ground. What do all of you think?"

The tribe looked around the cave and looked at one another, but had no answer. They knew that splitting into groups would be the best plan, but they wanted to be able to stay in contact with one another.

Oren expanded on his original idea to help remedy this situation. "Seff, I want you to walk two hundred paces forward in the center path. I will take the left; Dov take the right."

"What are you planning?"

Before he could answer Kabos, Almon already understood what Oren wanted to do and explained it to the others. Oren wanted to see if Seff and Dov could hear each other through the cavernous walls.

"How will we know to come back if it does not work?" Dov asked Oren.

Oren paused for a moment to collect his thoughts. "If you two cannot hear me, then I shall come back and shout down your corridors for you to rejoin us."

Seff picked up his torch before walking down his corridor. Oren went down his corridor next. Then Dov. Almon, Gurion, and Kabos waited in the silence for the three to return.

"Seff," Oren shouted to the right-sided wall, "can you hear me?"

"You are faint and somewhat muffled," he shouted back to the left. "Can you hear this?"

Seff knocked on the left wall. "What am I supposed to be hearing?"

"I was knocking on the cavern's wall. Guess you did not hear it. Stay there for a moment."

Seff moved over to the right wall and called to Dov. "Lummox! Can you hear me?"

Dov moved to the left side. "Barely, but I can hear you."

"Stay there for a moment."

Seff moved back to the left side. "Oren?"

"Yes, Seff?"

"The oaf can hear me."

"Good. Seff, I am going to count to five. Then I am going to yell over to Dov. Tell me if he hears it."

"Fine," he said with a bark as he quickly went back to the right wall. He pricked up his ears as Oren shouted over to Dov. A few seconds later, Seff shouted to his youngest brother. "Lout?"

"What is it?"

"Did you hear Oren just now?"

"Oren spoke?"

"Yes. Hold for a moment."

Seff once again moved back to the left wall. "Oren, he did not hear you."

"All right, Seff. Tell him to go back to the group, and you do the same."

Seff yelled over to Dov with Oren's instructions. The three began to make their way back to the rest of their small group. The cavern lit up as Seff emerged from his corridor first. Dov made his way second; Oren came last. They walked forward and rejoined their kinfolk.

"Were you three able to hear one another?" Almon inquiringly asked.

"Well," Dov spoke with hesitation in his voice. "Only if we were shouting. Our regular voices did not work. Oren and I could only hear Seff, but Seff was able to hear us both.

Oren looked among the gathered pack, "What do you wish to do? If we are to split into couples, then the two in the middle would have to be the mediators for the rest of us."

The clan looked around and argued amongst themselves. Almon wanted to split up to cover more ground, as did Kabos, but Gurion thought it unwise, as they had only one pathfinder.

"If we are to break into three groups of two," Oren said, "we need to balance them."

Seff exhaled heavily and spoke. "Oren, if I go down that center corridor again, whoever comes with me is being the mediator. I do not run back and forth for people's amusement."

Kabos had some slight worry in his voice now when he spoke to the group. "What would happen if one group finds the prize?"

"The greedy one makes a good point, Oren," Seff said.

Oren looked toward Kabos. "Those who find it would call out to the other groups who would then have to backtrack and make their way down the proper tunnel."

"Great plan."

"Quiet, Seff," said Kabos.

Gurion turned his head over to Oren. "What are you thinking for the groups then?"

"As Dov, Seff, and I are familiar with the corridors we have traversed, we will keep with ours. Gurion, you go with Seff. Almon, go with Dov. Kabos, you will come with me. Each pairing will have their own torches. Does anyone have any questions about this?"

The group looked at each other and thought it best not to argue about their respective partners. They all agreed in some form or another that Oren was working hard at keeping the balance among them and ensuring they all work together to find the prize and another way out of the cavern. Seff began to make his way toward the center path until Oren stopped him. Oren walked over to Gurion. He handed him a jar of preserves. He then went to Almon and gave him the same.

"All right, we can go now," he said before walking back to Kabos.

The six walked up to their separate tunnels and looked around at each other, wondering if they would ever set eyes upon one another again. They breathed in and began walking, two by two by two. As Oren followed Kabos, he unexpectedly shivered. He wondered what this uneasy feeling coursing through him was. He stopped for a brief moment and pondered. He knew it could not be that the small band was being followed, as the cavern was sealed behind them. Still, he peered behind him to make certain. He could not see anything there. As the group split, Oren shook it off as nothing more than nerves, but he still felt deep down in the pit of his stomach that something was just not right. He turned back and anxiously ran forward to catch up with Kabos.

Day Twenty-one

Seff was drudging forward like a dead man, with Gurion out of sight behind him. Seff only knew he was there because of the dim light reflecting off the walls, which he could faintly see out of the back corners of his eyes.

Seff stopped and mustered all of his strength to shout over to Oren. "We need rest. Oren?"

The pairs were doing fairly well keeping near to each other, despite the barriers found on both sides. Still, they were not completely lined up with themselves, so, when it came to conversation, it took some time for their words to be relayed to one another. It took Oren a few minutes to answer Seff, but a shout eventually came from the left wall.

"Tell the others to stop. We will make camp here."

Seff threw his torch forward toward the ground and looked at Gurion. "You heard Oren. Let the others know."

Gurion shouted over to his younger brother. Dov and Almon stopped in their tracks and had a seat on the ground as they shouted back over. Gurion relayed their message to Oren and Kabos. Now that the group had stopped, Gurion sat down with his back to the cavernous wall.

As he rested his arms on his knees, he asked, "What are we going to do for food, Seff? We ran out five days ago. It is a good thing we have some water left with us, even though it is stale."

Seff looked over toward Gurion. "Would you rather be drinking your own urine like everyone else is doing for sustenance?"

Gurion quickly shook his head no. Seff laughed. "Remember Kabos losing control after two days without water about how we would not survive?"

Gurion remembered the day Seff was talking about. Seff continued before Gurion had a chance to answer the question. "I believe Kabos would have lost his mind had it not been for Oren calming him while we asked Almon what he was doing. Thank heaven for Almon and his logic. I was becoming tired of hearing Kabos make deals with God."

Gurion agreed with his elder brother, but, once again, he brought up the subject of food. Seff looked over at Gurion and licked his lips. He withdrew his blade and made his way toward him. "Seff, what are you doing?"

Seff grabbed Gurion's russet-coloured mane with his left hand and cut off a chunk of it with his right. He showed Gurion the clump of hair in his hand. "It is a good thing you have a lot of hair around your head, brother."

Seff opened his mouth and placed the hair inside. Still chewing, he asked, "Would you like me to cut some more so you can have something in your stomach, brother?" Gurion agreed. Seff sliced and handed his brother a piece of his own hair. Gurion was reluctant at first to resort to eating a piece of himself, but, when his stomach grumbled, he opened his mouth and swallowed.

"Seff, I have a question for you."

He rolled his eyes. "What is it?"

"Why are you tough on Dov? He is your brother, as he is mine."

Seff grunted. "He is a dimwit who has had everything handed to him on a dish. I was the first. Mother and Father learned firsthand with me. When you came two years later, they were better. Unlike Dov, you were intelligent, and you could provide for yourself at an early age, so they did not have to worry. Dov latched onto Mother and always looked up to you. His size may have helped you plow and keep the fields at home while Father and I were our separate ways. Other than that, what has Dov done to show his worth?"

Oren and Kabos were sitting across from each other, one flame in between them and one flame behind them. "How are you faring, Kabos?"

"I am fine, although I wish we had some food."

Oren nodded in agreement. "I cannot wait until we get out of this cavern," Kabos said. "I believe the first thing I will do is purchase myself some pleasurable company. There is this one cute girl that my sister works with."

"How is your sister doing?"

"She is well. She has managed to avoid having a child in her line of work, which is quite impressive. How about you, Oren? How are things with your girl?"

Oren smiled, fondly remembering her delicate features. "Good. We have been talking about starting a family."

"Really?"

Oren nodded. Kabos laughed.

"You should enjoy it now because once you have some children—"

Oren interrupted Kabos. "I am not certain that would happen."

Kabos leaned forward toward Oren with renewed interest and anticipation. "You? Indulging before marriage? This is the last thing I would have expected to hear from you." Kabos smirked. "How good is she?"

Oren smiled once more. "Well—"

"Dov?"

"Yes, Almon?"

"To keep my mind off these hunger pains I have been feeling, as we have not eaten in six days, I have a question for you."

"What do you wish to know?"

Almon placed his torch down. "That conversation about Oren never eating flesh has been playing over in my head. I am the newest member of your group, and this is not the first time all six of us have been together, though I am curious to how it began. The five of you appeared close on the evening that I met you. I remember walking into the tavern for a meal three years ago. You were sitting at a table eating fish; the other four were on stage. Oren was playing some instrument that I cannot recall. Kabos, Gurion, and Seff were drinking and trying to sing."

Almon sat beside Dov after marking the cave wall. Dov looked at the inquisitive Almon. "It did start before my time so I can only recount to you what I know from what others have told me before I was included."

"That is fine," Almon anxiously told him as he wanted to hear the tale. "Take all the time you need." Dov looked into the flame resting before him and collected his memories. "In the beginning, there was Seff, Oren, and Kabos. They had met one day when a traveling scholar started taking on new students. They had many instructors over the years, as some came and went to teach in other areas.

Almon was intently listening. "The three of them were chosen, along with five or six others that day. Gurion was around at this time, but he was still learning how to walk. He was not allowed outside of the house without Mother or Father. God only knows why, but those three quickly became good friends."

"So that is how it started. Now I understand how close they have been over these years that I have known them. Suddenly, the talk of that tutor before we entered this cavern makes sense."

Dov shook his head up and down. "They only had that tutor for a year or so. Gurion never studied under him but the two did meet on a few occasions. After a couple years, Gurion joined them in their studies with different tutors. Only Oren finished all of the teachings. Kabos was the first to leave. It was not because he did not enjoy the teachings. They taught him nothing about business; Kabos has always had an eye for currency and wealth.

Almon chuckled. "So I have noticed."

"Gurion once told me that Kabos was leaving his teachings early to view the traders in the marketplace and gain knowledge firsthand. Seff was next to leave. Our family had a rough time financially when I was five years old. Seff used this as an excuse to travel abroad and look for work while Gurion stayed at home on the farm. Seff left for the first time with Father when he was twelve. A couple years later, Gurion abandoned his teachings."

He explained to Almon that his mother didn't allow him to go to his teachings when his time came. Dov came to know Oren and Kabos from the times he walked with Gurion to his lessons. Oren would also go over to help on the farm when things were rough, which further acquainted the two.

"Every time Oren came to help, Mother would insist he stay for a meal. On occasion, Kabos appeared with Oren. He sometimes tried to sell us items or appraise what we had. Mother fancied him in an unusual way. As I grew older, Gurion taught me, as I was around him all the time. Mother sometimes sneaked off to some place she would never tell me about as I helped Gurion on the farm. When Seff was in town and the marketplace was not busy, we would all get together and celebrate. Oren never drank spirits or ate flesh, but he did enjoy himself. We met you that night of my sixteenth birthday, and you know the story from there."

Dov took a few seconds. "Almon?"

"Yes, Dov?"

"I do not fully understand why Oren gathered all of us together. Looking for an ancient prize does not seem like him."

Almon took a moment to think before he answered. "Oren is a provider. He thinks of us as part of his family, so, when he found that map, he realized it would benefit us all. Being in this cavern for some twenty-odd days was not part of his plan. None of us thought we would be in here this long. If we knew that, none of us would have come, except perhaps Kabos."

Dov smiled at Almon. "That does make sense."

He looked away from the flame and over to Almon. "Tell me, what was the reason for you becoming cast out of your village? All this time has passed, and none of us knows why."

"It is not something I like to talk about." Almon smiled hesitantly. "But you told me your tale, so I will tell you mine. It began after the second harvest of the season six years ago."

Day Twenty-four

"Gurion, did you hear that?"

"Hear what?"

Seff paused and waited. "That! There! It sounded as if it were a squeak."

"Yes, I heard it. What do you suppose it is?"

Seff did not answer. Instead, he started to run forward with newfound energy. Gurion was behind him, keeping pace.

"Maybe it is a rat or some other creature we could kill and eat."

Seff drew his weapon. As he continued running forward, he started to notice a faint light ahead of him. "Gurion, there! Ahead of us. There is light!"

Seff and Gurion ran faster until they reached the light where they stopped.

"Oren? Kabos?" asked Gurion with a somewhat dumbfounded look on his face.

Both tunnels had come to an end. The four companions found themselves in an area as wide as they had been in before they entered their separate corridors. Seff and Gurion looked over at Kabos and noticed he had his index finger up to his nose and over the middle of his mouth. Seff looked at Oren, very perplexed. Oren brought his torch out into the open and pointed to the ceiling. The ceiling was much higher than it had been in the other areas. Seff looked carefully and noticed the ceiling contained some movement to it.

Seff licked his lips and spoke in a hushed voice. "Bats."

Kabos looked toward Gurion and noticed the few patches of what remained of his hair. "What happened?" he whispered.

Gurion pointed to his stomach and then swallowed. Kabos understood. A hand reached from behind and startled Seff. He turned around and noticed it belonged to Almon. Dov's and Almon's tunnel twisted to the left and merged with Seff's and Gurion's. The pair missed it as they were running toward the then-unknown sounding squeak. Gurion turned around and saw his younger brother. Dov was so happy to see him that, when he embraced him, Gurion could barely breathe.

Dov let go and stepped back. "Brother, your hair!"

"Dov, be silent," Gurion whispered as he held his index finger to his lips. He pointed to the ceiling. Both Dov's and Almon's eyes followed his finger.

"Whoa!"

Almon surveyed the room after seeing the bats. He found the doorway to the next corridor and pointed to it. It was to their left in the middle of the wall to the wall across from them. Almon began moving toward the archway, but Oren stopped him.

"Hold, Almon. What are bats doing this far in?"

"Perhaps there is an exit nearby," Almon replied.

Oren could not help but feel some uneasiness. If there was an exit nearby and the bats were resting near it, then salvation would soon be theirs, but, if there were no exit then, what did the bats know that drove them so far into the cavern?

Seff rolled his eyes. "Does it matter why they are here? They are here, and so are we. Now we have a chance of an actual meal. We would be mad if we were to pass this opportunity by."

The others looked at Seff. "What are you talking about?"

"The bats, Dov. We can eat them. A feast hanging in wait above our heads. We shall draw them downwards and kill them with our blades."

"How do you plan on bringing these creatures down?" Kabos asked.

Seff shrugged his shoulders. "I do not know." He turned to Oren and Almon. "Ideas?"

The two quickly came up with a plan. Oren walked to the center of the room and placed down his torch. He motioned everyone over to do the same. The six flames brightened the cave when they were all concentrated in one spot. The small tribe of six could see the walls from one end to another.

"Why are we doing this?"

Almon looked to Gurion. "In order to help us see and avoid injury. We will make loud noises to wake them and send them into a panic."

The six spread out and placed their backs all around the circular area so they would be far enough apart as to not hurt themselves. Everyone took in a deep breath as Oren put three of his fingers up and started to count down. Seff licked his blade with feverish excitement. When Oren's fingers were all down, the clan screamed at the top of their lungs with their voices aimed toward the bats, stirring them from their rest. A dark cloud came forth from the ceiling's stalactites and enveloped the room. The shadows moved around in a frenzy throughout the open area. The bats were scratching and biting while the tribesmen were swinging their weapons around aimlessly. Shadows started falling from the wall's grace as the tribesmen felled bat after bat with their swings. After a few moments, the only shadows that remained were of the tribesmen and the bats who had not escaped. Some of the bats were still moving, trying to rise up and fly with only one wing or screeching as they lay bleeding to death on the ground.

"There must be one to two hundred here!" exclaimed Dov with delight.

They all went around, sticking anywhere from four to eight bats on their weapons before sitting around the fire, except for Oren, who took his seat last.

"Are you not roasting bat, Oren?" asked Kabos.

"I am fine. Enjoy your feast."

Gurion asked, "What will you eat then?"

Seff laughed. "Yes, Oren, all we have to eat is bat now since Gurion has little hair left."

Gurion looked to his right at Oren and tapped the top of his head with his free hand. "Remember, Oren, I have to grow my hair back. It may be some time until your next meal."

Laughter erupted from the assembly. Dov leaned over and looked at Oren. He took off the first bat on his sword skewer and offered it to him. "Come, Oren, you have to eat something. You have provided for us over the years, and now it is our time to provide for you."

Oren told Dov to keep his bat. He stood up and walked across the corpse-ridden battlefield. It took him a minute or two before he skewered his own victory meal. He went back to the fire and sat down next to Dov and Kabos. He placed his sword over the open fire. He turned his head to the left and then to the right.

"It appears we have solved our food problem for the next couple days."

The covenant erupted in laughter once again as the flame's shadows flickered in harmony with one another.

Day Thirty-three

The six were now in a corridor that was steadily declining downwards. The tunnel's roof had lost a few feet compared to the other tunnels. Dov felt this hindrance more than the rest of the group. The rest of the tunnel, however, had widened enough now so three could stand side by side with enough space between them and the walls to remain comfortable. Seff was front and center with Kabos and Almon to each side of him a few feet back. Oren, Gurion, and Dov were lined horizontally behind them.

Kabos turned his head right. "How many godforsaken days have we been down here, Almon?"

Almon continued to look straight ahead. "I no longer know."

Seff stopped and turned. "Who gives a damn on how many days we have been in this godforsaken hole? Why are you so concerned about time, Kabos? What does it hold for you?"

Seff walked toward Kabos and got right in his face. "Trying to see how many deals you have missed out on? Is that it? Who cares? What is it that you have to get back to? Are you losing money without being in the marketplace? Come. Tell me! Tell us! Why is time so important to you?"

Dov stepped forward and pushed Seff back. Seff held his ground against his youngest brother. "The dimwit is standing up for something. Do you think that your size scares me?"

Dov slapped Seff across the face before he had time to react. Seff laughed. "A slap? I see that, by spending all that time attached to Mother's legs, you did not learn how to fight properly."

Dov knocked Seff to the ground with a vigorous push. He pointed at Seff and shouted. "Leave her out of this, Seff. You do not know her!"

"I do not think any of us know her half as well as Kabos does here. Is that not right, Kabos?" Seff held his stomach as he rose from the ground with Oren's help.

Dov looked at Kabos, who was now turned toward him. "What does he mean, Kabos?"

Seff laughed hysterically. Dov pushed Kabos back forcefully. Gurion stepped in front of his younger brother. "Calm down, Dov."

"Do you know what Seff is talking about?"

Gurion nodded. "I do, but it is nothing to concern yourself over."

Dov formed a fist. Gurion noticed this. "Dov, you do not want to do this. I am quicker than you."

He brought his arm back, but Gurion quickly knocked him upside the head. Dov fell to the ground unconscious. Gurion looked to his left. "Seff, why did you have to bring that up?"

Seff laughed. "I still cannot believe he has not figured it out by now. How slow can one be?" He looked over at Kabos, who held some worry in his face. "Do not worry, old friend. I do not blame you for anything. Father was gone often. I would rather it be the devil we know laying with Mother than someone else."

Oren spoke with some frustration in his tone. "Look what you started, Seff. We now have to wait for Dov to wake up before we can continue on."

"I know that." Seff kept his back to Oren.

"Can we not just carry Dov over our shoulders?" Kabos asked.

Gurion looked over at Kabos. "It would take two of us."

Seff looked over at Almon, who was inspecting the wall of the cavern and missed everything that had just happened. "Almon, what are you doing?"

He did not take his eyes away from the oval-shaped rock wall. "I have found something very interesting written on the wall here."

He motioned for the others to come over to him. Gurion peered over Almon's shoulders and toward the wall. "What is it?"

Almon ran his hand down the rough cavernous wall. "It appears to be a symbol of a serpent wrapped around a harvesting scythe."

"What exactly does that mean?"

"It means that other people have been here before, Kabos," Seff answered. "If they have survived this far in, then perhaps we are near an exit."

Kabos' eyes widened. "If that is true, perhaps that means the prize left with them and this hell we have been living through has been for nothing!"

"Kabos, calm yourself," said Gurion.

Seff began to smirk. "Yes, Kabos. For all we know, an entire city of cave dwellers exists inside this cavern. A whole civilization nestled away, lost to us, the above-ground dwellers."

"Wait one moment."

The group looked back toward Almon.

"Despite how questionable an idea that is, if Seff is correct, then that must mean there is a water source in this tunnel system. You cannot have an entire civilization living on urine, can you?"

"If we decide to search for water," said Seff, "we will have to find it soon. We ran out of bat and their flesh and blood for sustenance God knows how long ago."

Oren looked down and pointed at Dov. "Someone will have to wake him or help drag him along with us."

Seff knelt down and slapped Dov's face a few times back and forth. He was still out cold. "Who is up for carrying this boor?"

Oren looked at Seff. "It is obvious that Gurion is needed, but I think you should help him."

"What help would I be, Oren? I am so scrawny."

"You should have thought of that before you started in on him. He may not be the most intelligent person, but he is your brother. Gurion will be holding most of the weight. You will do fine."

Seff scowled at Oren with his eyes as he stood up. "Who will lead then?"

"I believe Kabos should. He is the most intent on finding this prize."

"Sounds reasonable."

"Quiet, Almon!" Seff said while he and the middle child helped their younger brother to his feet.

"Kabos," Oren said, "take the lead."

Kabos enthusiastically jumped towards the front of the group and called to them. "All right, everyone. Follow me, and we shall find this prize!"

They continued their journey forward with Kabos first in line. Behind him were Oren and Almon with the three brothers trailing behind in the background. They walked for almost an hour until Kabos suddenly slipped and fell on his back. His torch landed in front of him. It rolled a few feet and began to make a sizzling noise. Kabos cried out in pain while holding onto his ankle. "My leg!"

Oren ran forward to check on Kabos. Seff removed himself from under Dov's shoulder and moved past the group after hearing Kabos' cries. Dov fell to the ground, and Gurion fell with him.

"Seff, how could you let us fall like that?" Gurion yelled toward him.

Seff paid no attention to his brother. He noticed a subtle film of water was on the ground, which was what had made Kabos fall. Almon and Oren helped Kabos up.

"Kabos, I want you to see if you can put some weight on it," said Almon.

Kabos stepped forward and winced.

"You should keep your weight off it," Oren said. "Almon, are you willing to help Kabos walk?"

Almon nodded in agreement. He tore a piece from the bottom of Kabos' tunic to wrap around the lower part of his leg before he put Kabos' arm around his shoulder. Oren walked forward and stood beside Seff. Seff pointed toward the cavernous floor.

"It appears that we need to be careful walking from here. There is slick moisture on the ground here, and it does not help that we are on a downward incline. Good fortune though. It means that we are either near water or an exit."

Oren pondered for a moment. "All right, Seff. I will help your brother and you lead once more."

This delighted Seff. Oren turned to everyone else and called their attention.

"The ground has some moisture to it. We need to take our time and watch our footing. "

They all agreed to be careful and take their time despite the thought of water or salvation. After Oren had placed himself under Dov's other shoulder, the covenant of six continued slowly on their way.

Day Thirty-five

The small tribe of six had stopped briefly to help Kabos rest his leg. Even though he was using his unlit torch as a walking stick, Almon was still helping him. Dov was once again stable and standing with the others. Seff took this few minutes of rest to bend over and lick the ground.

"How can you do that, Seff?"

"I am sick of drinking urine after every couple of sleeps, Oren. I would rather absorb this little moisture with my tongue despite the dirt."

He dropped his torch to look for more. As he moved forward, a sharp and sudden slant made him slide down a tunnel. The others ran over, except for Kabos, who hobbled with the wall's help, as they heard Seff's voice quickly fade down the hallway. They found the sharp slant and looked over it. They realized that, if they slid down there after Seff, there would be no way to get back up.

"Seff," Almon shouted down, "are you okay?"

Seff dusted himself off. "Yes, I am fine."

"What do you see?" asked Dov.

Seff rolled his eyes in the darkness. "I cannot see anything although—" He sniffed the surrounding air. "I do smell something fresh."

Kabos quickly picked up the torch Seff had dropped and sent it down the slide after Oren commanded him to do so. Seff was ready for the torch as he saw the light coming down the tunnel. The torch continued past him. Seff watched as it rolled around the room before coming to rest.

He faintly noticed some clear liquid in the distance. "By God in heaven. Water!"

Seff quickly and instinctively ran toward the water hole. He started drinking as if he had never tasted water before. This water hole found within the center of the newfound cavernous area, which could easily house two to three hundred persons, was deep, yet it did not flow. It was, however, fresh and tasted very cool. The water hole itself appeared simply as a natural circular chasm that seemed to have no bottom within the rock floor. After hearing Seff's cries of finding water as well as the echoes of his tongue lapping in as much as he could, Oren stood up and backed away from the slant before running forward and diving on his belly to slide down. The others followed him in some form or another, sliding either on their bottoms, backsides, or bellies. They all left their torches where Seff's was laid and joined him. They drank until their stomachs could hold no more. They refilled their empty preserve containers and drinking flasks with water as Kabos wet his leg bandage. They laid there panting with exhaustion for a few moments before finally getting up and reclaiming their torches to explore their vast, new sanctuary. The six wandered around the area separately.

Dov was the first to speak. "This place is huge! What do you make of it, Almon?"

Almon paced around and took in the new environment. "This place seems to be an air pocket. The water seems to be coming from a source under the cave. We must be very deep underground by now."

They continued to roam around the rocky, stalagmite-filled lobby for a few minutes. As they explored, they discovered five different tunnels that led out from the sanctuary. Kabos found his exit near a rocky, little hill. Seff found his on the right side of the watering hole, far off in the distance. Gurion found one on the ground level to the left of the water while Dov found another next to a tall rock pillar. Oren found his last, and it lay just past the watering hole. Almon, who was scanning the walls, found something much more interesting.

"Look here. I have found something!" Almon called to the others.

The clan of six made its way over to Almon's light.

"What do you make of this, Almon?" Kabos asked.

"These cave paintings appear to depict people, but I cannot decipher what they are doing."

Almon moved in closer to the wall and walked with it to the right as Gurion went to the left. The clan looked around and noticed many other stalagmites, rocks, and columns lining the floor in a sporadic fashion. Almon continued to observe the faded images while he made his way around a couple pillars until he suddenly stopped. "I have found that serpent scythe symbol again."

Gurion called over from his side. "It is here as well, although it seems to be above what appears to be a shepherd's cane lying on the earth."

Seff stated what everyone was starting to realize. "Paintings surround this entire pocket."

"It appears as such," Gurion replied. "This is troubling."

They heard a sudden cracking sound. Dov lifted his foot and was taken back. "It has become worse."

The others looked over at him while he bent over. He picked up a bone from within a pile found near him. He threw it into the center of the sanctuary. The bone appeared to be human, most likely from that of a leg. The assembled inspected it.

"This is not a good omen," said Gurion.

"If you think that is not a good omen, brother," Seff started. "You are not going to like this."

Gurion looked over at Seff and noticed him holding a skull near his face with his right hand. The white, yet dirtied, skull shone brightly in the darkness due to the torch in Seff's left hand. Kabos looked down near where he was standing.

"I have a skull here as well." Kabos took a moment. "At least these people did not obtain our prize."

Gurion called over to Kabos. "I think we have bigger problems than that on our hands now."

A voice unknown to the covenant of six suddenly echoed within the cavern. "I bid you six welcome."

The small gathered tribe looked at each other in the dimly lit lobby.

"Who said that?" Oren asked.

The men looked at each other in silence.

"Quit fooling around!" Oren forcefully demanded.

"None of us said anything, Oren," said Dov.

Seff drew his sword. "Then who did?"

No one had an answer.

"Draw your weapons and form a circle," Seff instructed. "We will be able to see from all angles." The group followed his orders.

"I like you," said the voice.

Oren quickly placed his right hand on Seff's right shoulder and whispered, "Seff, listen. This voice seems to have an affinity for you. Keep it talking so we can figure out from where it is coming from."

Seff nodded to Oren. "Who are you?" he demanded to the darkness. "Show yourself, you coward."

Laughter filled the pocket. The companions knew the voice was coming from one of the exits they had previously found, but could not tell from which.

"A coward it says. How funny!"

Seff barked. "What do you mean by it?"

The voice laughed again. "Come now, puppet. Do not become upset."

The other five found the exit from which the rambling voice was coming from and took position around the cavernous doorway.

The voice tauntingly laughed from behind them. "Not that way, gentlemen. You will never find me if you continue down that path."

The tribesmen became baffled and looked at each other.

Gurion worked up some courage. "What are you? How did you come to be here?"

The voice spoke again, coming from yet another direction. "I am in a giving mood. Allow me to share a secret with you all. I did what it was I had to, what was right for I was wronged and discarded for my humbled and gracious offer for another's. An offer brought forth from a man who constantly sought approval from those around him. How I despised that man. I would commit that act once more on him if given the same chance for it is I who was truly blessed, not him."

Almon took a stance and raised his voice as he stepped forward. "Did you commit the same act on those whose remains are scattered among us?"

The voice came from behind them again. "Would you think I would be so vain as to kill those who enter this holy shrine? I do not murder anyone who enters this cave, especially those who make it this far. We are hidden from view you see. Nothing can see us or our actions in this cavern. I brought in those remains you found here. One cannot have the tunnels crowded with waste. Many have died during this process. Those bones are of the most recent."

"Why did you not help them?" Oren asked.

"I misjudged them earlier." The voice came from the exit nearest the rock pillar Gurion had found. "They were not worthy of such a precious gift."

Dov whispered to the rest of the group. "How is he doing this?"

"He must know the layout so well that he is able to throw his voice in different directions," Almon answered quietly.

"No one knows that I dwell within this cavern, but I thought it would be more beneficial this time if someone knew of my presence. I have never seen a group as large as this make it this far. You may be dismayed, but you all do not look nearly as troubled or weak as those smaller groups that have made it here. In light of this, allow me to tell you something that will lift your spirits high."

The clan listened.

"There is an exit to this cavern."

The tribe looked around at the exits they had recently discovered.

"Where? I will not tell, but know you this. You could not have come at a better time. You would have all perished outside this cavern, as the rest have, if you had not come when you did. I knew it was only a matter of time before some catastrophe such as this happened. I am delighted to see that it was you who found my map at the right time."

Gurion fiercely questioned the voice. "Your map? What are you talking about? Stop speaking in riddles."

The voice laughed at Gurion's attempt to frighten it. "Yes, it was my map that one of you must have found to lead you to the entrance of this cavern. It is good to know that greed still exists in the world, no matter your own personal reasons you had for coming may have been. Wealth or power. Passion or thought. No one realizes their own greed to the full extent."

The six friends looked at each other and pondered what this voice meant within its riddles.

"Humility is the purest form of greed. The timing of your lust, gentlemen, could not have come at a better time. Unlike those previous experiments who unwittingly stumbled in before you, those who fell haplessly with their blood and screams echoing throughout these rocky, blackened halls, you have purpose. You are chosen ones."

Seff leaned over toward Almon. "What exactly does he mean by experiment?"

Almon shook his head from side to side. He had no idea. This newfound variable took him aback.

"You have always been chosen ones. You are life's vessel. That is your providence. We will show who is superior! Yes, we will! If, by some chance you should happen to fail and die in this cavern as those who came before, I will have more blood and colours to help finish painting the shrine you see before you."

Dov looked over at Oren. "I do not wish to become a cave painting."

"To think is to be caged. To be caged is to see. The answer lies before you. The others who have come before did not see." The voice paused briefly. "If you are hungry, there should be enough insects under the rocks in this chamber for you to regain your energy. Remember to eat sparingly. Food is hard to come by in this cavern. I wish you good fortune, gentlemen. It may be some time before we speak again."

Almon asked what this was supposed to mean. No voice from any direction came to answer him. He asked once again.

"The voice is gone, Almon." Seff withdrew his sword. He turned toward Oren. "What do we do now?"

"What choice do we have, Seff? It did say there was an exit." He looked from side to side. "Were could it be?"

Kabos interrupted, "It did not say anything in regards to the prize."

Seff looked at Kabos. "Do you still believe that there is an ancient prize? We have been set up by this … this voice."

"Perhaps, but the voice must come from a person, right?" Kabos asked. "Does it sound familiar to any of you?"

Everyone shook their heads no.

"How does it survive down here? It even said there was not much food within this cavern. I think it has the prize and preserves with it."

Almon spoke in Kabos' defence. "Kabos does make sense. Still, what are we going to do? There are five exits, perhaps even more that we have not found yet within this chamber."

They assembled into a circle after Almon's question and talked for hours amongst themselves, as they had a lot to take in. They concluded they would uproot some stones, eat, and store some insects away in containers before resting for the night. After waking, they would start down the path that was above the small, rocky hill.

Day Forty-seven

The tribe of six had made their way up a steady incline for a few days now. They continued to traverse the high-roofed tunnel, which could hold them two by two by two, but they were not in this pattern. Seff was single and still leading the group while Almon was single in the back with the rest in the middle in two pairs of two. Seff suddenly put his hand up and stopped the clan.

"What is it?" Gurion asked him.

"Take a look."

The clan peered over Seff's shoulders. The tunnel opened a little, and a land bridge was seen. The left and right of the tiny bridge held no ground, only a darkness that seemed to never end as they peered down into it.

Seff huffed. "There always has to be a problem."

"We have no other choice than to cross it," Oren stated firmly. He looked toward Seff.

Seff knew what Oren was about to say and answered him before he had the chance. "I am to be first to cross this small bridge?"

"You are the pathfinder, are you not?"

Seff grunted at Oren and started to make his way carefully across the tiny bridge. He placed his torch between his teeth so he could see as he crossed. He outstretched his arms to better hold his balance. The assembled watched Seff anxiously as he successfully crossed.

"Who is next?" He joyously shouted over to the rest of the clan.

Oren stepped forward and crossed. He kept his torch in between his teeth just as Seff had, but made the crossing appear much easier. Limping very slowly as his leg had still not fully recovered, Kabos made his way across third. The group watched in horror as he almost lost his balance a few times, but he finally made it across to the relief of his friends who had been watching from both sides of the pit. Gurion followed suit, but he didn't lose his balance as his predecessor had. Almon kept his torch in his hands as he didn't even outstretch his arms during his crossing. The five looked over and beckoned Dov to come join them.

As Dov was preparing to cross the tiny bridge, Seff whispered, "This will be difficult for him."

Oren nodded. "Everyone be ready."

"Remember, brother, do not look down," Gurion yelled from across the pit. "Keep your eyes focused on us."

Dov started to cross. He knew his size was an infraction to him so he made his way very slowly across the pit, slower than even the injured Kabos. He noticed the ceiling and stood at full length. He held his torch in his right hand and outstretched his left arm for balance. After ten long, anguishing minutes, Dov had only crossed the bridge halfway while the others watched with horrid anticipation. As Dov took another step forward, he lost his footing. Scrambling and with much determination, he was able to regain his place quickly and avoided falling into the deep darkness. The five who had made the crossing all sighed in relief. Dov continued to make his way slowly across the pit. He was almost at the edge when he lost his balance and slipped. To the five watching, it appeared as if he were falling in slow motion as his torch fell into the abyss. Seff leaped forward without a thought for himself as his torch fell to the side of the cliff. His hand grabbed Dov's outstretched and frantic arm.

"Do not worry, Dov. I have you. Hang on."

Seff began sliding across the ground toward the pit because his youngest brother was so big and heavy compared to him.

"Seff!" Oren screamed. He dropped his torch behind him and grabbed onto Seff's legs.

Seff was now completely over the cliff's edge. Oren was starting to be dragged down into the pit after him. Gurion grabbed onto Oren's legs and became the anchor for the other three. Seff was holding on as tightly as he could while Oren was halfway over the edge, bending like a tree branch in a heavy wind. Both Kabos and Almon held onto Oren for his support while Gurion continued to hold the chain. All five remaining torches were scattered on the cavernous floor.

"Brother, do not let me fall!"

"You will not fall! For God's sake, hang on!"

Seff looked into Dov's eyes. "Steadily pull yourself up over me and grab the edge. You are strong! I know you can do it."

"I ... I ... cannot ..."

"Do not speak like that! Focus!"

Dov brought his left arm over to Seff's shoulder and started to climb. Oren sank further down into the darkness. The heads of both Almon and Kabos started toward the pit because Dov started his climb. Gurion took a stance with his right foot forward to better hold his grip without being tugged as he used the archway of the next tunnel for leverage.

"Good. Now place your other arm over my other shoulder."

Holding on with his left arm, Dov removed his right hand from Seff's left in order to swing it over his brother's other shoulder. He unwittingly built some momentum and attempted to use this to secure his grasp onto Seff. Instead, he lost his hold over his brother's right side. Scrambling, his other hand was able to grab Seff's left. He did not have a good grip and as his left arm dangled, he began to slip.

"Dov, listen to me. I will not let you go. Place your left hand in my right. It is my stronger arm."

Dov frantically tried to grab Seff's right as he was slipping from his grasp. Almon let go of Oren and took his satchel in hand. He passed it down to Oren before he grabbed onto him again. Oren proceeded to let it fall over him so it came to land in Seff's right hand. Dov lost his grip from Seff's left arm, but grabbed onto the satchel hanging from his right. All that was keeping Dov from the darkened pit was the satchel's strap. Dov began swinging back and forth like a pendulum, due to the momentum he lost after losing Seff's grip. Seff's eyes locked with those of his fear-filled brothers.

"Gurion, start pulling backwards!" Seff shouted.

He did so very slowly and cautiously as to not break the chain with any sudden movements. Oren was no longer hanging halfway over the ledge.

"I have you brother. Hold on," Seff told Dov with reassurance.

The well-worn satchel began to rip.

Dov's eyes widened as he heard the tear in the dark. "Brother!"

"Do not worry, Dov."

"Gurion, pull faster!" Seff commanded.

The satchel continued to tear. As Gurion was pulling backwards, Dov kept trying to grab onto his oldest brother, but he could not latch on to him due to his swing. Oren had been pulled back far enough now that the only part of him hanging over the edge was his arms that were holding onto Seff's legs. As the satchel continued to tear, Gurion, with all his might, kept pulling backwards. Kabos grabbed onto Seff to help Oren in case he lost his grip. Almon reached over the edge and outstretched his arms so Dov could perhaps grab one as he swung back and forth. The sound of the satchel tearing was the only noise that could be heard in the darkened cave. Dov desperately tried to grab at the three hands that were welcoming his, but he could not reach them. Seff looked into his brother's eyes as the satchel's strap finally gave way. Dov's bloodcurdling scream resonated among the cavernous halls as he fell into the darkened pit, vanishing from the tribe's sight.

"Brother!" Seff cried as he was pulled back onto solid land. He leaped back toward the pit, but Almon stopped him by blocking his path.

"He is gone, Seff."

Seff gave Almon a push toward the wall. He was holding his right arm under Almon's chin. "No, he is not gone!"

Gurion paced around in disbelief. "This cannot be happening!" He looked at Seff and screamed at him accusingly. "You let him fall, did you not? You let him go! You never cared for him!"

Gurion picked Seff up by the throat and pushed him up to the wall. Seff squirmed.

"I did not let him fall!" he whimpered.

Oren grabbed Gurion's shoulder. "It is true. I saw everything. Seff tried his hardest to save Dov."

Gurion continued to hold Seff while he looked back over his own shoulder. "How do you know? Did you see the intent in his eyes?"

Oren firmly stood his ground despite Gurion's ferocity. "No," he stated calmly, "I did not have to." He stared into Gurion's eyes. "Believe it. Seff tried to save your brother."

"How can you know that? You are not around us all the time!"

Oren turned his head and looked down the chasm while he answered Gurion. "Seff may not have cared for him, but he did love him in some form. Would he have leapt forward without concern to himself if he did not? He leapt before you."

Reluctantly, Gurion let Seff go. He had nothing to say in regards to Oren's comment. He quietly made his way over to the edge of the chasm and cried out at the loss of his brother. Seff crept up behind him and joined his lamentation. The remaining three companions gathered around the two brothers and the surrounding darkness. They all mourned in their own separate ways in a collective moment of silence at the loss they now had to acknowledge. They said a prayer for his soul. Even the faithless Almon said Dov would be delivered from evil and placed before the Almighty One to be judged fairly. After the tears were shed and hymns given, the new tribunal of five picked up their torches and continued on their way through the passageway.

Day Fifty-five

The pack had reached the zenith of the current path's height a couple days after Dov had fallen into the darkness. The path was curving now, and it had a steady slant downwards. As Seff was moving the clan forward, he noticed what appeared to be a faint light, flickering as a reflection off the cavern's walls from the oncoming distance.

"What is that?" Kabos asked.

The clan moved quickly forward in anticipation. They exited the tunnel and found themselves in a large chamber.

Gurion shouted, "Is this—"

They looked around in disbelief as they were back in the pocket chamber of stalagmites, rocks, stone pillars, and accompanying water hole. The light they came to see was from the torch that Dov had dropped as he fell days prior. They turned their heads and noticed the exit they had just come out of was the pathway that held a rock pillar before it.

"This ... this cannot be!" Kabos cried out.

Seff had a seat on the cavernous floor. "The path was nothing more than a circle." He began to laugh hysterically. "Dov died for nothing."

Oren saw the outline of what appeared to be a figure in the background. While the others were bickering amongst themselves, he moved in for a closer look. He was horrified at what he saw. It was Dov, impaled on a stalagmite. The protruding spike was bearing through his chest cavity. The massive rock spear was stained with blood that had dripped down from the body after it had become skewered. Oren raised his right hand and placed it over his mouth. If he had anything in his stomach, he would have thrown it up. He called over to the rest of the small tribe.

"At least he did not suffer," Almon stated.

Gurion, who was standing next to Oren, said, "It would appear otherwise."

"Think on it, Gurion," Almon replied in a logical way. "If Dov hit the ground as opposed to becoming impaled, even though it is quite doubtful, he may have survived. If he had, he would have become shattered and broken, unable to move, laying there in constant, agonizing pain until his end."

Gurion knew Almon was right, but it was more the sight of his impaled younger brother than Almon's words that were forcing him to fight back his tears. Oren looked over at Almon and gave him a very dirty look that he noticed in the dim light.

"He did not suffer this way. He went peacefully," Almon said once more. "I believe this was the better of the two possible outcomes."

Seff tackled Almon from out of nowhere and landed on top of him. His torch fell to the ground and rolled close toward the water hole. Seff's hands were gripped around Almon's collar as his saliva spewed forward while he yelled. "What of the fall? He could not have fallen peacefully knowing he was bound to hit the ground. Your eyes were looking down as he fell. Tell me what you saw in his eyes!"

Oren and Kabos pulled Seff off Almon and restrained him. He was too aggressive to hold back so they let him go, which allowed Gurion to grab and hold his brother back. Seff began struggling. Oren walked in front of him and started to talk him down from his crazed state.

"Almon was only trying to help, Seff. Tell us that you do not prefer instant death opposed to a slow one constantly filled with pain."

Seff was frantically shaking his head to help free himself from his brother's grasp. Gurion placed more pressure on his hold.

"Oren is right, brother. Almon was only trying to ease our pain. It did not work on how he went about it, but you cannot blame him for trying."

Seff stopped struggling after he realized it was useless, and Gurion let him go. He ran over to Almon, who was still lying on the ground. He stood over him silently in the almost nonexistent light produced by Almon's torch, resting a few feet from him. Seff reached for his sword with his left hand before outstretching an open palm with his right.

"Choose."

Almon looked at Seff's hands. He placed his right hand into Seff's opened palm. Seff helped him up. He eyed Almon very closely. "Do not try to ease my pain further!"

Seff put his weapon away and turned to face Gurion. He pointed toward the rocky spear. "Let us get him off that rock."

"Right, brother."

The two blood kin took opposing ends of the stalagmite and started to push Dov's back upwards. Rib bones were heard scraping against the solid rock as they started their lift. The body began making a squishy, reverse suction-type noise as it continued to be slowly ripped from the rock skewer. Kabos covered his ears at the sound; Almon shut his eyes. Oren watched before going over to give a hand to Seff when the body began to be too high for him to continue. Finally, they got the body off and placed it down next to the small, rocky, hilled entranceway. Seff wiped the sweat from his brow and made his way over to the water hole, which they had since coined "the well," to pick up the torch. His eyes widened. He called for Oren to join him while the others dealt with Dov's body.

"Yes, Seff?"

Seff pointed toward the well. "Was the water this low when we left?"

Oren looked down, following Seff's hand. He crouched over and took a closer look while placing his arm in the water. The water was still deep, but had receded a little. Almon called over to them.

"What is happening there? You two are fairly quiet."

"It seems as if the water is receding," Oren responded.

Kabos had a look of extreme worry on his face. "What?" He hobbled quickly over to the water hole with every container of his in tow. He started filling them frantically while on his knees.

Oren pushed him back so that he fell. "Calm down, Kabos."

He looked up. "We cannot run out of water, Oren. It is bad enough we finished the food from the last time we exited this chamber."

Oren motioned to Gurion. Gurion agreed and went to pick up one of the randomly placed torches. He began lifting some rocks to find more insects. There were very few, but he stored them away in containers before he walked over to the group.

"These are all the creatures I could find."

Kabos went from worried to horrified. "See? Do you see? What will we do for food?"

The covenant of five agreed that Kabos was right. Food was going to become a much larger problem than the current recession of the water, as they could still easily refill their containers. They separated and began looking around for more small animals and insects.

"I am marking the entranceway to the connected path we finished traversing with a small, sharp rock," Almon shouted as he searched.

After a few moments, they made their way back to the water hole and formed in a circle to show what little they had found. They knew it would not be enough unless they picked the proper channel, as they still had three paths left to explore.

"If only we had something large with meat on its bones," Kabos thought aloud.

The assembly looked at each other very slowly around the bright, gathered flame at the same time as if they all had the same morbid thought. They looked into each other's eyes and saw the agreement within as they thought the answer too ghastly to speak. They looked over and started making their way over to Dov's body, swords drawn and fire held ready to cook.

Day Sixty-one

The tribe was still in the pocket chamber, slowly taking away flesh from the body of Dov. Gurion and Seff were seated a few feet directly across from each other. Oren was further up, almost as if he were on point. They were trying to come up with a plan. Kabos was sleeping off to the side of this triangle; Almon was pacing back and forth, inspecting the walls.

Gurion turned his head toward him. "Almon, leave the wall alone and sit down. Your movements are beginning to make me anxious."

Almon had been trying to decipher the paintings on the walls for the past few days while the others were trying to recover their strength as they planned. He became a man obsessed. He would only wake up, examine the cave paintings, eat a little piece of Dov, and then go back to sleep. This particular day, he was fixated on what he thought looked like a field, running back and forth between other paintings, looking for some connection to it.

"This may be the best chance to understand this cavern." He squinted as he continued to inspect the wall. "If we should, we may be able to escape sooner rather than later."

"We shall figure it out soon enough. Sit and eat. Dov is turning worse," Gurion said in an attempt to get Almon seated. His words did not tear Almon away from the wall, so Gurion turned his head back to the group to continue with their conversation.

"We cannot split into groups," Oren said. "These passages are placed further apart. Our voices will not be able to carry as they had previously."

"That voice also said the answer lies before us. It would be wise to stay together," remarked Gurion.

Seff asked the question on their minds. "Which is the correct path?"

45

Oren pondered for a moment and remembered the voice also said to think and see. "Almon may be onto something with his wall speculations. Remember what the voice said. To think and see." He shouted over to Almon. "Have you found anything?"

"I have found something of interest. This painting of a field before me looks as if some tiller is on it, but what is interesting is that the field is red."

The tribunal stood up and made their way over to Almon, watching their footing as they stepped over Kabos and scattered mounds of bones and rocks.

"A field should not be red," Gurion commented as he drew closer to Almon.

Seff looked at Gurion. "One does not have to be a farmer to know that, brother." He looked to the wall. "Perhaps it is just painted as that was the only colour the painter had."

Almon brought the torch closer to the wall. "Look." He pointed to a small piece of the field.

From this section, they could see a base colour underneath the red field.

Seff brought his nose up next to the wall and sniffed. He recognized the smell instantly. "The red on the field is old, dried blood."

They decided to split up and examine the walls more closely.

"Is there anything of significance there, Seff?" Gurion asked his older brother.

"There appears to be a shape of either mud or clay. How about you, brother?"

"The serpent scythe symbol is repeated constantly. Almon, have you found anything more?"

Almon nodded. "I see a tree surrounded by a meadow."

He asked Oren if he had found any other paintings.

Oren did not respond. He was silent as he was running his left hand across the wall. They walked over to the light that was emanating from his torch. When they reached him, they noticed him placing his left index and middle fingers to the wall before taking them off and rubbing them with his thumb.

"This picture seems fresh. It is still drying."

The companions looked at themselves dumbfounded.

"How can that be?" Gurion asked. "We have not left this chamber for God knows how long. Surely we would have seen or heard it being done."

"Unless," started Almon, "that being who can throw his voice creeps in here as we sleep and adds to his shrine."

"What does it look like?" questioned Seff.

Oren looked up from his fingers and over at him. "I do not know. I have not given it a proper look."

Oren turned around and brought his torch closer so they all could see. The portrait had a triangle with a person lying on his back stuck in the middle of it. A few inches away from that was another triangle, but, this time, no one was placed on it as if they had been skewered. Instead, five people were sitting around a fire with what appeared to be pieces of the impaled man's body in their mouths.

Gurion gasped. "Is that us?"

"Do you know of anyone else who was impaled from a jagged rock, only to be taken off and eaten by five others, brother?"

"That voice person has to be watching us," Almon said.

"Who or what is this thing?" Gurion nervously asked. "How is it able to watch us while we are awake without us noticing? It would—"

Oren interjected. "Whatever or whoever it is, we need to figure it out as soon as possible."

Almon placed his right thumb under his chin and bent his index finger under his nose.

"He said this was his shrine. There must be something here to do with him."

The others agreed with Almon's reasoning.

"What do we currently know?" Gurion spoke of the serpent and scythe symbol as well as the red field that contained an image of a tiller with it. Oren commented on the tree surrounded by a garden. Seff brought up the shaped image that appeared to be either mud or clay. The four looked at each other, trying to piece it together as they stood in a circular pattern.

Almon spoke first. "There are many images of nature … tree, meadow, and field."

"Clay or mud is natural too," Seff told him. "It is of the earth."

"True, Seff," Almon responded. "Though, mud is not a pasteurized symbol. Things cannot be grown from it."

"Almon," Gurion said as he quickly looked at Seff, "we have worked on many fields back home. A field is not completely natural. You plan where you plant things."

Seff agreed with a nod of his head. "My younger brother makes a good point. Additionally, there is a tiller and a scythe, symbols of a harvester taking away the naturalness of the world. Trees and meadows grow in their places. One can cut these things down, but they are not planned ahead of time, especially on how large they may grow. You can only predict it."

Oren snapped his fingers to call their attention. "Forget the clay and harvesting. Why is the field red? That is what I wish to know."

"Oren is right," Gurion said. "That is unnatural. Something must have taken place in that field."

Seff looked over to his brother. "Gurion, what would turn a field red besides murdering some creature and having it bleed out onto the ground?"

Immediately, Gurion, Seff, and Oren looked at each other in epiphany.

"No, that cannot be him," Gurion said.

"Who could it be?" Almon asked as he did not pick up on what the other three had realized.

"The marked one," Seff told him.

"Marked one? Who are you speaking of?"

"He who killed his brother," Seff continued.

Almon's eyes opened wide with realization. "That is a story. It cannot be true."

"Doubt it if you so wish, Almon," Oren told him. "Clay and a meadow with a tree. A harvesting scythe with a serpent wrapped around it. A tiller in a bloodstained field. It points toward him and how we came to be from that garden."

"It is a shame no one has plunged a sword into his gut," Seff said. He drew his weapon. "I will see to it that he falls unto mine."

Laughter pierced the sanctuary. Kabos was awoken from his sleeping state because of this.

"A blade cannot kill me," the voice said. "A fairly blind man tried with an arrow once. He was hunting for his dinner and brought his son along with him to act as his spotter. I deliberately acted as an animal from a distance to draw them near. When I was struck, I fell over and laid there motionless as they approached my supposed lifeless body. Seeing they apparently killed a man and not an animal, the man was grieved for having taken an innocent life. He killed his son, the spotter, because of this. The man began to make his way home to his loving wives, though he would not have made it without aid due to his poor vision. I disguised myself as a traveler and came to assist him to his home, where he insisted I meet his family."

Oren looked up into the darkness lingering over his head. "Why did you decide to help him when you did not help those others who have entered this cavern?"

The voice chuckled. "My plan is divine in purpose."

"And what plan is that?" Oren asked.

"All in good time. All in good time."

Gurion roared. "Oren's question is sound! Tell us now!"

There was no response. Silence reigned with the exception of the crackling fire from their torches.

Seff lost his temper. "He is beginning to irritate me," he said through gritted teeth.

Kabos looked over to his four companions. "What happened?"

Oren looked back and over at Kabos. "While you rested, we made several discoveries."

He updated Kabos on the events that had just unfolded. They began to talk and concluded they needed the voice to help them if they were ever going to survive and find their way out. There was only one problem. They did not know how to summon it. They figured they should go about their business, as it seemed it interjected at pivotal times.

With a new plan and path ahead of them, they went back to Dov's body. It made a sickly peeling noise as they tore what little flesh remained from its bones. Almon placed the meat under his torch to smoke it so it would be better preserved, even if it would be just a couple of days longer. Seff bent down, detached the right femur from the rest of the body, and placed it in his hand for use as a club. They made their way over to the well. They bent over and refilled their containers with water.

"Think this will be enough?" asked Gurion.

No one was longer sure.

"Wait!" Seff spontaneously exclaimed. "I have an idea."

He walked over to Dov's body. He picked up his brother's skull and had himself a good look, face to face. He took the femur and smashed open the top of the skull. He walked back to the well. He tore off a piece of his tunic and plugged the orifices just in case any water would leak downwards from the bowl section from the back of the skull. He placed his hand in the water and submerged the skull. He brought it out of the water and had himself a drink. The remaining four were quite impressed.

"Good idea," Kabos said. "There must be plenty of skulls for use in this chamber." His tone suddenly held some worry. "Will the water not become stale fast? We have no way to cover them."

Oren looked to Kabos. "We will drink from the skulls first and then from the reserves. Despite the taste, the stale water will keep us going."

Kabos felt like an idiot for missing something very obvious. The group split up to look for more skulls. After a few moments, they returned around the water hole with an additional three containers. Seff used the femur club to open the skulls and handed one to Gurion and Kabos. Being one short, Almon and Oren decided to share. They submerged their glasses. After the skulls were filled, they stood with torch and skull in hand as they looked at the exit that lay before them just past the water hole. They began to walk forward, down the unknown path, hoping to see if it would lead to their salvation.

Day Seventy-five

The corridor they had entered fourteen days ago was a long, winding one. Despite this, the path had no inclines or slants, nor did it have any alleys that broke away from it. The same went for the rock ceiling. It was steady and constant with no stalactites or protrusions coming from it. There came a rumble from one of the tribesmen.

"Gurion," Seff said viciously, "tame your stomach!"

With annoyance, Gurion said, "Brother, do you not think I have been trying?"

Seff barked back at him. "I am surprised that it has not eaten itself by now."

"Quit your bickering!" Oren forcefully told them. "We do not need any additional reminders to eat."

Kabos offered a suggestion. "We need a distraction."

"What should it be?" Gurion asked.

Seff's eyes looked up toward the rock ceiling. "To continue with what we do not have in this cavern, the first thing I am going to do when I get out of here is to pay a visit to Kabos' sister. It has been far too long."

"It is quite funny how she makes more than Kabos," Oren joked. "I can understand though. It is a most welcoming profession."

Seff laughed and spoke humourlessly. "What would your mother say about your mouth lately, Oren?"

"Speaking of mothers," Kabos interrupted, "how is yours these days, Seff?"

Seff smirked. "She is well. Not that I have a problem with that, but what of the woman your sister works with that you have been mentioning?"

"I would rather your mother. It is a sure deal, and she has much experience."

"Your sister's friend does not?"

"Yes, though—"

Gurion's voice came from behind, cutting off Kabos. "Leave him, brother. You know he does not wish to pay."

"I know." Seff chuckled. "It is a good thing Dov is not around to hear this. If he found out some of Mother's tricks, he would have your head, Kabos."

Oren smirked, but tried to conceal it by shaking his head.

Seff caught this action out of the corner of his eye. He started walking backwards so he was facing Oren. "Come, Oren. You cannot tell us you will be leaving that bedroom of yours with your woman once you get home."

Oren held his smirk, but tried not to blush. Seff turned to face forward once again. "Perhaps since Kabos will be with Mother," Gurion said, "I will have that woman he has spoken of."

Kabos spoke backwards over his shoulder. "Take her, Gurion." He looked to Almon. "What of you, Almon? I am sure we can obtain you one. My sister works with many different women."

Almon did not answer Kabos.

Oren looked over at Almon. "Almon, you have been very quiet lately. What is the matter?"

Almon's face was slightly tilted down toward the floor. "Nothing. I am not very talkative today."

Seff did not let Almon's answer go. He couldn't. He directed his voice backwards toward Oren. "Have you not noticed that, since we found out who the voice was, he has been in a state of reflective thought? The faithless man has proof of faith now, and he has no idea how it should be dealt with."

Almon remained silent. Seff stopped walking, halting their advance.

"Come to think of it, we do not know why he had no faith to begin with."

He turned around and faced him. "Why is that?"

Almon said nothing. Seff was not expecting an answer to his question, but he was sure it had some painful memory to it. He turned forward to take his lead. The others started walking behind him once more. Oren looked over and smiled at Almon.

"Ignore him. We will buy you a pint when we get out of here, and you can regale us with the story if you wish."

"Thank you for the offer, Oren, but I think that pint will have to come after the pleasures of the flesh."

Oren laughed and spoke jovially. "Remember, now that we have proof, we cannot gratify each other or ourselves. Else, it is eternal damnation for wasting our seed like that."

The rest of the pack smirked or laughed in their own little way after hearing Oren's words.

"Unfair, Oren." Kabos responded sarcastically. "Taking yourself off the marketplace with potential buyers near is no way to turn a profit."

He smirked. "I am a valuable item, am I not? My handsome build, hazel eyes, fine, blonde hair that leads eyes astray. It is a burden I gladly bear."

All that could be heard now was the laughter that erupted from the covenant as they continued merrily down their path, free from their hunger pains.

Day Eighty

The group exited the tunnel they had been traversing, only to find themselves back inside the chamber cage. As before, the path turned out to be one way and looped around.

"Again?" Seff shouted in anger. "I do not believe this!"

He dropped his torch, took out his femur club, withdrew his sword, and started frantically attacking the walls. Gurion could see quick glimpses of his older brother in the darkness as sparks emanated from the blade as it struck the wall. Almon fell to his knees and began to cry while Kabos approached the well. He leaned over the edge to cleanse his hands as he thought them dirty, not because they had run out of water. He noticed the water had receded even more since the last time they were there. Kabos outstretched his arms to full length, and he was just barely able to wet them. Oren walked over to Kabos. Gurion made his way toward his frantic brother. In an attempt to snap some sense into him, Gurion grabbed his brother's shoulder from behind. This startled Seff, and Gurion took an elbow to the face. His torch fell to the ground. Enraged and without thinking, Gurion retaliated by picking up his brother and throwing him against the wall, knocking him unconscious. Regaining his wits, he grabbed Seff's collar and dragged him past Almon and over to Kabos and Oren, leaving the two dropped torches burning on the ground where they laid. When he reached the others, there was a distraught silence.

Oren spoke to help give his troupe some confidence. "Keep your spirits high. Only one path remains. It must hold our salvation."

Almon stood up and wiped the tears away from his eyes. The others also began to cheer up.

"Oren must be right about that," Kabos said.

Gurion was looking down the well. "How will we be able to replenish our containers when we can barely reach the water?"

Almon looked around for Dov's clothes, seeing how they did not eat those. Once he found them, he made his way toward his companions. "We can tear these into strips and form a chain to lower the containers into the water."

Gurion threw a pebble into the water to show the rest how deep the well was. "That is fine in theory, Almon, but would it not be too fragile to reach the water? We do not wish to lose any containers."

Almon didn't have a response. He realized Gurion was correct. Kabos was intently staring at the clothes.

"I have an idea," he said.

Kabos stood up and made his way to Dov's bones. He tore the spinal column from the body. The crackling sound of ripping bone echoed within the chamber.

"Almon, can you bring me another ribcage complete with spinal column?"

Almon looked around until he found one. He brought it to Kabos. After tearing away the second spinal column, Kabos bound them together by tightly fastening sections of Dov's clothes to the joints. Once he was finished reinforcing it, the two spinal columns coiled around his feet as he held it waist high from his hand.

"Look!" he decreed. "An extended arm."

Almon, Gurion, and Oren were speechless.

"Why are all of you staring at me? You have all witnessed firsthand the items I have fashioned from household objects and sold as priceless artifacts in the markets."

"Kabos," Gurion said, "that is remarkably clever, but how are we going to hold the containers in place while we attempt to fill them?"

Kabos scratched the top of his head as he pondered. "That is a valid question, Gurion."

Almon looked at one of the two ribcages and extended on Kabos' idea. He snapped off a few ribs and bound them to the sides of the bottom of the extended arm. He took a small container, placed it in between, and fastened more of Dov's clothes to it. To make sure the container didn't decide to float away after they would submerge it, Almon fastened some tinier bones from the skeleton, such as fingers, around the neck of the container and attached it to the spinal arm to better hold it in place. He reinforced the bindings and slowly started to lower the extended arm into the well. After a moment or two, he brought the spinal arm back toward him. The container was filled with water. Almon unbound the container, put the lid back on it, and placed a new container in. He had to redo all of the bindings for each container, sometimes even tearing new clothing strands to use as the old ones dried by the combined torch light. It became a very lengthy process. He looked at the others.

"After we finish filling these, we should leave this chamber. As Oren has said, only one path remains."

"We should take a night to look for food and gather our strength," Oren suggested.

"Additionally," he said, "this will allow Seff to recover from Gurion's blow."

The covenant wished to move forward and suggested they carry Seff, as they had carried Dov when he was unconscious, but Oren said they needed a pathfinder, which put an end to the rising debate.

He turned to Gurion. "How did you knock Seff unconscious?"

"I do not truly know. He elbowed me in my face, and I reacted instinctively. He may have hit the wall in an unusual matter."

Almon finished filling up the last container as Gurion spoke. He placed the extended arm next to the water hole. The clan spent a few moments on an insect hunt before they closed their eyes for some much needed rest.

Day Ninety-one

The covenant was walking forward. Seff noticed something that seemed quite unusual. There was light up ahead, but it was not daylight. This light was actually from their torches reflecting off the cavern wall in front of them. It was a dead end. Seff dropped his torch and ran forward. He lividly scratched the wall up and down as if he thought he could dig through it. The ends of his fingers quickly became stained with blood as some of his nails were being torn off due to his furious clawing. He sat down and started to laugh hysterically.

"No way out." He laughed again. "There is no way out of here. None at all."

The others watched him, but stayed far enough back just in case he was going to do anything unpredictable.

"The answer ... the answer lies before us. That is what he said. That is what he said!"

Seff stood up and ran toward the pocket chamber, pushing his friends aside and leaving his torch. His babbling could be heard as he hastily made his way through the darkness. Oren picked up Seff's torch.

"What are we to do now without our pathfinder?" Kabos asked.

Oren sighed under his breath. "He may be rambling, but his words do hold some truth. Seff has the right idea. We have no other choice than to head back to that large chamber." Oren turned and looked to his left. "Gurion, how long will Seff be able to keep his haste?"

"God only knows. We will not be able to catch him unless he collapses from exhaustion."

"We might as well start heading back to the pocket chamber," Almon stated.

With only four of them now, they turned around and started back toward their desolate sanctuary. Almon took the lead. Kabos and Oren stood side by side in the middle as Gurion brought up the rear.

Day One hundred

The tribe of four were coming to the entrance of the pocket. As Almon stepped out first, he was brought to the ground from a clubbing blow to the back of his head. Seff was hiding off to the left on the other side of the naturally constructed oval doorway. He jumped forward and swung at Kabos and Gurion. The force of his surprising blow knocked them both backwards and to the ground. Seff bent over and drew his blade. He positioned it over Almon's throat after kicking him over so he was on his back, as opposed to being on his stomach.

"Seff!" Oren shouted as he brought himself into the sanctuary after stepping over Kabos and Gurion. "Do not do this!"

Seff stood up and turned his rabid, hungering gaze toward Oren. "We need to eat. Yes, we do. There is no way out of here. None. I intend to live as long as I possibly can." Seff walked toward Oren. "Do you think you will be able to stop me?"

Oren threw the torch Seff had dropped nine days prior with his left hand and then dropped his own with his right before drawing his blade. One of the torches burned Seff's left arm, but he did not feel or notice the pain.

"Seff, stop this at once. Working together is the only way to ensure our survival!"

Seff laughed and took the first stab at Oren with his sword, which he was holding in his dominant right hand. Oren parried this attack, but Seff was dual-wielding. Oren was struck across the face by the femur club in Seff's left hand. Oren was brought back with what was to become a huge bruise on his cheek.

Seff laughed once more. "It appears that Dov is more useful in death than he was in life."

He rabidly started at Oren again. In the background, Kabos and Gurion had gotten to their feet. They saw Seff attacking Oren. They threw their torches ahead of them so it would help illuminate the chamber even more. The two drew their swords and ran toward Oren. They took point around Seff and had him trapped inside a triangle. Seff stopped his attack and shifted his eyes amongst the trinity.

"Brother, cease this foolishness!" Gurion pleaded. "You cannot win against the three of us."

Seff kept shifting his hazel eyes. "You dare to challenge me, dear brother?" His eyes came to rest on Kabos and he smirked. "I gladly accept."

He rushed forward. Kabos blocked both the attacks from the femur club and the sword, but he was knocked down as Seff gave him a kick to the stomach. Kabos dropped his sword as he hit the ground. Oren raised his blade to bring it down on Seff's backside, but, before he could, he was brought to the ground from an elbow to the face. Gurion tried the same, but Seff was able to bring the club to his back and denied his brother from landing his blow. Seff did a quick turnaround hop with his blade extended and cut through the midsection of his brother's tunic, tearing just enough through to expose his chest. Down but not out, Kabos grabbed his blade. He was on one knee when Seff noticed he was getting back up.

"Your taste for currency has always disgusted me," Seff screamed.

He gave Kabos a quick foot to the head, knocking him to the ground once more, as he was parrying his younger brother's ferocious strikes. Oren was back to his feet. He slashed at Seff's legs, but he jumped over the attempt. As Seff was in the air, Gurion gave a downward slash, but Seff dodged and riposted with the femur club. Gurion spun around and fell to the ground with his arms stretched outwards to help break the fall. Kabos was slinking away to the water hole as Oren fought with Seff. Seff pushed forward with frenzy, and Oren was barely able to deflect the whirlwind of attacks. Gurion attempted to come to Oren's aid.

"Brother," he called, "stop this madness!"

Seff turned his head to Gurion and laughed hysterically. "It is too late for that, dear brother."

Seff was standing between Oren and Gurion. Oren and Gurion looked into each other's eyes in the dim light and decided to attack at the same time. Despite being between them, Seff was still able to deflect and dodge their unison of attacks. Suddenly, there was the sound of a crackling twang as something struck Seff across his face, something that caused a fair-sized gash on his already heavily scarred face. Seff took his left fingers and touched his face. He brought the blood from his fingers onto his tongue and looked over at Kabos, who was standing there with the spinal arm coiled near his feet. He removed the bindings that held the containers in place, and he was using it as a whip.

"Now is our chance," Oren said to Gurion.

The two quickly took their points once more. Kabos attacked Seff, but Seff brought the femur club up to protect himself. The spinal whip wrapped itself around the club. Seff smirked. He was about to pull Kabos forward with a tug, but Oren brought his blade down across Seff's right arm. Blood jutted forward and started to stain the floor. Kabos used this distraction to jerk the femur club out of his hand and bring it toward him while Gurion slashed Seff across the backside. Despite all this, Seff was still standing.

"Fools!" he cried in his hysteria. "Have you not realized that we are all dead? We have been for our entire lives!" He punched his brother in the face with his good hand even though it was clutching his sword. Seff turned and used his right leg to knee Oren in the stomach. He quickly brought his right elbow down on Oren's back as he was hunched over from the attack to his abdomen. Seff scanned for Kabos, but another lash across the face greeted him instead. His head was forced to the left and toward his brother. Gurion gave Seff a blow across the face with his right fist, forcing him to spin and stagger into Oren, who was on one knee. Seff's eyes widened as his belly slid into Oren's strategically placed blade. Oren let go of the hilt and fell backwards. Seff's weapon fell from his hand as he looked at the blade in his gut, which ran clear through to his backside, with shock as he held it. Oren, Gurion, and Kabos stared at him. Seff suddenly pulled the blade out and clasped the hilt. The three could not believe what they were witnessing as crimson flooded from him. Seff raised Oren's blade above his head. Before he could bring it down on its former owner, he fell to his knees and collapsed onto the hard cavern floor. An amused and delighted voice entered the sanctuary.

"Very exciting, gentlemen."

Oren, Gurion, and Kabos looked up from Seff's corpse.

"You certainly know how to entertain." The voice paused for a second. "It is a shame that one with such recently discovered potential had to die though, even if it did take three of you. I am glad you found my map. I could never have imagined the riches you have brought to the table."

"What are you talking about?" Kabos yelled. "There is no prize here!"

Gurion and Oren sighed at the fact that Kabos was still using the aspect of finding an ancient prize to keep his mind stable and off the problem before them.

"That is where you are wrong, pupil."

Intrigued, Oren started to listen more closely.

"The prize stated on my map would be you."

"What are you talking about?" Kabos asked.

"I used the map to bring you to me and preserve the treasures of this world."

Kabos fell over and started to shake. Gurion went to check on Almon as Oren conversed with the voice.

"All you wished for was entertainment? Is that the reason for your map?"

The voice laughed. "No, this show has been an added delight. I had hoped that one you just murdered would have made it out alive, but things do not always end the way you hope them to. Life is full of surprises at times."

Oren's voice rose forcefully. "Then why create the map? Why repeatedly drag people down here?"

"It is a game of sorts."

"We die, and you win? Is it that simple?"

"There are no winners or losers to this game, puppet. No heroes or villains. That is not what this is about."

"Tell me what it is about then."

"It is about influence."

Oren was growing frustrated. "Make sense for a change!"

"It has taken untold years and preparation to set this into motion. From luring those not of my lineage down to this cavern to securing one of my blood aboard that vessel during this disaster, hoping these events will culminate into one precise moment."

"What is this disaster you keep mentioning?"

"It does not understand. It has shown the capacity, but still does not understand. The outcome will be most beneficial for the cause. It is almost over. When it is, no matter how painstaking it has been over the years, all the experiments before you and your group arrived, will have been well worth it. Wait and see."

Oren did not understand. "Why do you not show us the way out? You seem to want us to survive this ordeal."

"I am not a coddler like God. Prove to me and yourself that you have the will and conviction for life everlasting, for that is what you will achieve if you happen to escape this sanctuary. People no longer see or comprehend. They become corrupted by interpreting his words to their own justifications."

The group made no sense of the voice's words. All they could do was continue to listen to its ramblings.

"I had an interesting conversation with the one you have murdered while he spent his last days alone in this shrine. He understood of the potential of man, the potential you have just displayed. He may have been temperamental, and it is a shame he was not able to bay back his madness. He taped into something divine and without pretext. Something God has been trying to right for quite some time now."

Oren took a few seconds to think. "You have taken it upon yourself to balance?"

"It is not about balance or defiance. I am not here to overthrow him. I have faith. The two of us share some of the same enemies and fight together against them."

Oren was no longer screaming. "Why have you spent all this time planning?"

"This is about perfecting what he has started. There is no quick solution to this problem, as he believes. It will not hold. He has his methods and I mine. Cage yourself and you will understand. The exit lies before you. Seek and you shall find. Liberation awaits."

"Wait!" Oren called out.

The voice disappeared once again into the shadows.

"Come back, you babbling cur!"

There was no response. Oren took a few moments and thought on the voice's words. He picked up his bloodstained sword, which laid next to Seff's body, and walked over to Gurion. "How is Almon doing?"

Gurion looked up at Oren as he was kneeling next to Almon. "He is not well. Seff struck him in the right place. He will not survive for long."

Oren drew his sword.

"Oren, what are you doing?"

His eyes shifted from Gurion and down to Almon. "I am going to put him out of his misery. Why let him continue to suffer?"

Gurion rose to his feet. "He is not conscious, Oren. How do you know he does not wish to suffer? Living is still living. Who are you to make that judgment call?"

"One who is looking toward the greater good. Your crazed brother was right. We do have to eat. If the voice speaks the truth in his ramblings, then salvation lays before us. We need to keep our energy high and look." Oren pointed down the well. "We need to construct a longer arm to reach the water when our reserves are up."

Oren pushed Gurion aside and slit Almon's throat. The blood flowed as a continual stream of tears onto the cavern's floor with a vile, gurgling noise. Oren's current actions baffled Gurion. He was watching his bearded friend die as he spoke to Oren.

"Oren, you are beginning to frighten me."

"I am, too, Gurion," he replied. "We need to survive. Once we find our way out of here, we will seek vengeance on that voice, which lured us here. Our fallen friends will have their rest. I swear this to you."

Gurion's spirits seemed to have lifted, even if just little.

"Come," Oren said. "Let us console, Kabos. I think that, if he has a drink and something in his stomach, it should ease his worries." He laughed. "It was only a matter of time until the great merchant Kabos was swindled due to his greed. Perhaps God is not without his own sense of justice."

Gurion agreed with him. The two sat next to Kabos. Oren offered their remaining friend a drink from one of his containers to help ease his worries.

Day One hundred twenty

The three survivors had finished devouring Seff by this time. They had to eat very sparingly as there was not much meat on his bones to begin with. They started slowly cutting up Almon, but the flesh was starting to turn despite their best preservation methods. They only ate from him if they absolutely had to and could not find any insects. Kabos spent his time making arts and crafts with the clothes and bones found in the chamber to keep himself distracted. He came up with a sort of bone lasso, something that would hold tight if thrown over an anchor of some sort. Kabos did not realize it could be used for something like that. He just saw it as a circle with a little nub that could attach to something else if tied properly.

He held it in his hands and stared. He could not take his eyes off it. Oren was looking for the exit. He was scanning the rock walls. Once again, fresh paintings depicting recent events were portrayed on them. He had started to deface them, but gave up shortly as they would always be renewed when next he woke. Gurion laid on his back, staring up at the ceiling he could not see high above him in the darkness and reflected on his ruined family. Kabos dropped his work and walked over to the water hole. He placed his torch down next to the well and had himself a seat. He looked at the now-longer spinal arm and then to Gurion and then to Oren. They were far enough away and paying him no attention. While he was sitting there with his legs dangling over the ledge of the hole, Kabos allowed his left sandal to casually slip off to see how long it would take to reach the water. He stood up as he waited. Oren turned around when he heard the splash. He looked at Kabos' face in the dim light that was making its way up from the floor. He knew what Kabos was about to do.

"Kabos," he yelled. "Do not leap!"

Gurion turned over and started slowly making his way over to Kabos as he stalked about on his belly.

"The voice has not been lying to us. I understand how to escape from this cage. I see it clear as the morning sky."

"Where is it, Kabos?" he soothingly asked, trying to calm him down. "Tell me where it is, and we can leave together."

"Death," Kabos morbidly declared. "The only escape from this cavern is death." He looked down the well. "I wish for my release!"

Oren noticed Gurion trying to get close enough to Kabos so he could grab him. He thought it best to keep him talking. "How are you certain that death is the only way out, Kabos? I wish to know."

Kabos paused to think. Gurion was almost within arm's reach.

"I do not know how, Oren. It is something profound, something I feel."

"Kabos, do not lose your faith on us. We will make it out of here."

"Just a little closer," Oren thought to himself.

"I have not lost my faith, Oren. I am embracing it."

Kabos took his leap of faith down into the well. Gurion tried to grab his leg, but he fell just short after his lunge. Oren rushed over to the edge as Gurion stood up. They looked down, but could not see anything. Instead, they heard Kabos' frantic splashing as he tried to keep his head above water. He was deliberately tiring himself out so he could sink beneath the surface and not suffer. Eventually, the splashing had stopped. All was silent once again until Oren spoke. "If he were going to take his own life, why did he not slit his throat up here?"

Gurion looked over at Oren, perplexed.

Oren continued to stare down the well. "We could have used some fresh meat. We could have used the bones to extend the arm." He shook his head. "Selfish to the end."

Oren paid no further respects for the next victim of the cavern. He left Gurion standing at the well and went back to searching for the way out of the chamber.

Day One hundred forty-five

Oren was sitting in the chamber with his arms around his knees, rocking back and forth while talking to himself. He became obsessed, trying to figure out the truth of the voice's message. "The answer lies before me. The answer lies before me. The answer lies before me. Dov is dead. Fell from grace. The answer lies before me. I murdered Seff. Before me. I murdered Almon. Me. Willingly. Kabos took his own life. Disaster … there is a disaster … but what? The answer lies before me. Cages … cages … we are in a cage. Cage myself within a cage to see. Pathways lead nowhere. Walls have no openings. Pillars are bars. I am the prize. I am the secret. I am life. Something is missing … something is missing."

Oren stood up and made his way to Almon's corpse. He sliced a piece of flesh with his sword. He opened his mouth, held his nose, and ate the rotted flesh. He went beside the rock pillar in front of one of the five exit pathways previously treaded a few moments later and threw up his meal into the accumulating pile that was awaiting him. Gurion was on his back, exhausted but still wide-awake. He could not sleep as he had been having macabre nightmares over the grim events that had previously taken place. He relinquished his thirst and hunger and lay next to the well with his intent to die. He had given up. Even though he had, he refilled all the containers with what little strength he had left for Oren to continue on, as neither of the two knew how much longer the water would last. As he drew his last breath, he rolled over on his side and closed his eyes for the final time.

Day One hundred fifty-three

All that was left now was Oren. The torches burning brightly next to the well displayed a hideous visage on the wall. The reflective shadow ravenously feasted on Gurion's fresher flesh, tearing and pulling away at the body without taking the time to slice from it. Crimson was splattering as it ate, staining its face and the face of the rocky wall near it. Somewhere in the darkness, a smile was forming on blessed lips while looming eyes watched the depraved scene with outmost enthrallment. The shadowy visage seen on the cavern wall paused briefly.

"Should be more tender," it said to itself.

It picked up the femur club and started to pound away on the slab of meat that lay before it. It worked up a sweat doing this to tenderize all those muscles, but was not thirsty. Its thirst was being quenched from the life force that once flowed through its friends' veins, allowing the precious reserves of water to remain untouched. Stopping, it placed its hand on the flesh in front of it. The meat had now been tenderized just to its liking. Before another breath could be taken, the visage went back to its holy feast.

Day One hundred seventy-seven

"It is almost time."

Oren was roused from his sleep by the whisper that sprung from the darkness.

He answered the voice in a daze. "What?"

"The time is nigh, puppet."

"Nigh for what?"

"For the pathway to become clear."

Oren began to rise to his feet. "Pathway? Your words will no longer mislead me, cursed one!" he said with conviction in his voice. "There is no way out of this cavern. It is only a matter of time before I die."

The voice interrupted Oren's lamenting speech. "One of your former friends unwittingly found the correct path."

Oren raised his head and looked about the sanctuary to which he had inhabited for so long.

The voice continued. "Though doubtful, he may have been able to make the passage in his state. Sleep tight, puppet, and build your strength. You will not be able to make the journey in your current condition with the state of the passageway. You are almost there. Almost out. Almost free. You always were my favourite student, Oren."

Oren could not believe the truth resounding within his ears. "No … you … you cannot be him … it … cannot be."

The voice deepened itself to a more familiar tone. "Rest assured I am. Long ago, I noticed something within you, a trait you exhibited more than these failed experiments whose bones litter the floor of this holy shrine. Remember my words, for we will not speak after this. The answer lies before you. Depart from this sanctuary and into the world I have provided for you. Satisfy your every desire, every wish you have with will and conviction."

The voice departed into silence, never to be heard by Oren's ears ever again.

Day Two hundred

Oren had been searching the cavern high and low for this exit, feasting on what insects he could find and trying to remember and retrace the steps of his friends. He fell into a fit of rage this day while pacing about the chamber and started screaming. The echoes of his maddening rants bounced back toward him.

"Who would have found the exit? Were they trying to prolong this misery? This agony? Why would they do that?" A sense of reason began to fill his mind. "No! They would not have done that. I have been listening to the ravings of a madman. A lunatic! A murderer!" He quickly spun around and raised his voice. "I am no puppet! I know you are there, watching from the darkness!"

Oren started to giggle hysterically. "Not a puppet! Not a puppet! Not a puppet! I lead my own life! My own way! My own way! You hear me?"

He made his way over to the well and kicked at Gurion's remains. They fell down the hole, and Oren turned away. He stood with his back to the well and breathed in heavily as if he were starting to hyperventilate as he waited for the splashing sound of the remains hitting the water. Instead, the remains made a crashing noise as if they hit something solid. Startled, he turned around and made his way over to the well. He peered down into it. He went over to one of the torches and picked it up. He dropped it down the well and watched it fall with childlike fascination. The torch spun as it fell, but the sound it made when it hit the ground resounded upwards toward Oren. The light extinguished a few seconds later, but the resonance was enough for Oren, who suddenly saw and understood. He picked up another torch and desperately started looking around for things he could use.

"What can I use? What can I use?" he babbled as he searched. "There must be something."

He knew that, if he just leapt down, he would not survive the fall. After a few moments of searching, he turned away in dismay and started to weep until something caught the corner of his eye. It was Kabos' bone lasso. He picked it up and looked around for a close stalagmite. He threw the lasso over the bloodstained impaler. He remembered where the extended spinal arm was and attached it to the lasso. He pulled on it to see if it would hold. It did not snap. He ran the arm to the well and down it to see how far it would go. It was way off. He brought the arm back up from the pit. He looked about for other materials that he could use. He remembered Almon's rotting corpse and made his way over to it. He took his blade and scrapped all the rotting flesh off it. The smell did not affect him in anyway as he had become accustomed to such things.

"His intestines look as if they could be used to lengthen the rope," Oren said to himself in order to help keep his sanity as he fiddled about Almon's corpse.

Even though he had sloppily removed the organs of his friends prior to dining, he was not sure of just how much decay had infected them, so he decided against it. He fashioned Almon's spinal column with the others. Seeing how that was not enough, he went over to the remaining bones of his friends as well as those of those poor unfortunates who came before them and took their arms and legs from them. He shaped them to the lengthening spinal arm before running it back down the pit. It was still not enough, but it was all he could use. He grabbed his satchel, filled it with what remained of the water-filled containers, grabbed a torch, and placed it in his jaw so it rested horizontally to light his way. He placed his hands tightly around the bone rope and began making his way down the pit. He tried to keep a constant speed as he did not want any sudden change to snap the rope or have it break if he lingered in place for to long. When he reached the end of the cable, he placed his torch in his right hand and dangled there.

"How deep is this well?"

Suddenly, he heard a crackling noise. He had lingered for too long. The constant weight at the bottom of the chain had caused it to fracture. The rope snapped, and Oren fell while the light from his torch trailed him all the way. A squishy noise reverberated as he landed onto something that broke his fall. Oren had landed on the soaked body of Kabos. He rolled off and laughed at the irony that had just befallen him in the darkness. There was no light to be found. The torch was extinguished as it landed in a small residual puddle. He used his hands to guide him as he felt around the walls.

Eventually, Oren found an archway. The path before him had a very steady incline, but he ran up it with unknown vigorous speed, nonetheless. The path evened itself out, and the light blinded Oren. He put his right hand over his eyes and continued his pace until he was finally out of the cavern. He fell to his knees with his hand still covering his eyes and breathed in the fresh air. Tears streaked his face.

"I made it!" he cried with outmost joy. "My fallen friends, your deaths have not been in vain!"

He slowly peeked through his fingers until his eyes became adjusted to the daylight. Once they had, he walked away from the cavern. As he walked, his sandals made squishing noises with each step. It was as if the ground was saturated with water from a heavy rainstorm or even that of a flood. In the distance, Oren noticed a lot of smoke in the sky. He could smell something that smelled like burning flesh as he walked forward. He found himself a hill and carefully made his way to the top of it. Not wishing to expose himself, as he did not know what was happening, he went on his belly and peered over the swampy ridge. He noticed a few horse carts on some soaked grass just outside an area that was mostly mud.

"Odd," he whispered to himself. "I see no horses nearby to draw those carts."

He spotted a most enchanting young woman making her way back to one of the carts. She lifted with all of her strength, pulled a body from it, and walked away. Oren watched her as she dragged the corpse. Her long, fair hair was blowing harmoniously in the cool breeze as she added the lifeless body to a burning mound of human corpses. It was as if she were cleaning up after a great disaster had befallen. Oren took his view back and noticed many other burning mounds. The mounds were each dedicated to one specific type of animal. The long, fair-haired woman made her way back to the cart and took out the corpse of an animal. She dragged it forward with the utmost urgency. She added it to the pile and started making her way back to the carts once more.

Even from a distance, Oren could tell she was exhausted. She was shambling forward, determined to finish her task, but she was too tired and collapsed. Oren made his way down the hill with haste toward her. He looked at her with a passionate hunger and noticed she had passed out due to overexerting herself in her task. He shook her to see if she would wake, but she did not. He tried again, but there still was no response. Oren then brought himself onto her. There, among the funeral pyres of the old world, he lay and satisfied his every carnal desire with her. After releasing his seed, he stood up and walked around the mounds, naming each species of animals as he passed. His eyes were fixated on the grotesqueries before him. As he walked about, he did not notice the stone that sat just before him. He tripped over it and fell into one of the mounds, catching fire. Oren frantically ran about and screamed for help, but quickly fell to the ground. He laid there on the soaked ground and burned as his life extinguished.

The woman woke up as the moon was shining down. She took one of the empty carts and walked back to a house. Outside, her husband was working while he waited her return. The rest of his family had already gone to sleep. She put the empty cart with the others. She made her way over to her husband and kissed his lips. He looked over at her.

"What kept you?"

"I fell asleep. This work is exhausting."

Her husband nodded. "We all agreed on the schedule."

"I know. Still," she said, looking down, "it nearly makes you wish we had not survived. You would think he would have the graces to clean the mess he started with this deluge, but all we are provided with is a … what was it called? A rainbow?"

The husband put down his work tools. "True. Though think on it." He placed his arms around her. "We were told to be fruitful and multiply. Every generation from here will be our descendants, either directly as sons and daughters or indirectly as nieces and nephews. Our piety is what made us chosen for this task."

She turned her head and kissed him a lover's kiss. In the darkness, the marked one's eyes watched his progeny take her husband's hand in hers as she led him into the house. He smirked as he knew she was already with child. The bloodline would survive and its new providence with it, masked to all by the veil of timing.

Ascendance

One

Mr. O'Brian looked at his screaming wife in the delivery room. "You really should have taken those drugs, honey."

"For the last bloody time, I want this to be a natural birth. No drugs are entering my system, you bastard!"

Evelyn, an obstetrics nurse at St. Joseph's Hospital, wiped the sweat from Mrs. O'Brian's forehead.

"You're doing great Mrs. O'Brian," said the doctor. "He's crowning. Just a little more. Keep breathing the way you have been, and you're as good as home."

Mr. O'Brian perked up as he heard the doctor's words. "Hear that, honey? Sounds like a textbook birth. You're really lucky for it to be going so well."

His wife gave him a cold stare. "Lucky! Lucky? We'll see just how lucky you'll feel when I make the end of your penis dilate to ten centimetres in width when we get out of here!" Mrs. O'Brian tilted her head backwards and screamed.

"See," her husband declared, "you wouldn't be in so much pain if you took the drugs."

"And run the risk of being numb and missing the orgasm?"

Evelyn and the doctor looked at each other, but said nothing. They both knew the general direction of where the conversation would be heading from here.

"You know that's just an urban legend, sweetie."

"Says you!" she screamed. "You wouldn't know when I'd have an orgasm to begin with anyway, you balding, sorry excuse for a male specimen!"

Mr. O'Brian's eyes started moving away from his wife.

Mrs. O'Brian continued her rant. "Your son will be more of a man in the Pleasuring a Woman department when he enters this world than you have been for your entire life! And don't fucking call me sweetie!"

Evelyn let out a small smirk in regards to Mrs. O'Brian's comment. She couldn't help it. She had never heard anything like that come from an upset, soon-to-be mother before. She tried her hardest not to laugh, but had to conceal it within a mock cough.

Mr. O'Brian hung his head to try to hide his embarrassment and slowly walked out of the room. He took a seat in the hallway, slightly off the side of the delivery room door. While he was sitting there, he turned his head and looked down the hall. He noticed two women walking about the otherwise empty peach-and-white hallway. As they were making their way from room to room, he noticed one had a clipboard. She was showing the other one around. He determined from her short, greying hair that she was middle-aged. Instead of being dressed in a nurse's smock, she was dressed in business clothes. As for the woman behind her, she was much younger, and she had amazing posture. She wasn't dressed in a nurse's smock either. She had on a pair of dark brown boots with two-inch heels. She wore a dark blue waist skirt, which was ruffled at the hemline. A raven-coloured sweater outlined her slender, trim figure. It ran down to her knees, adding a charismatic presence to her aura. The sweater was left open and exposed a button-down silk blouse. Her soot black hair was hanging in a single braid running past her shoulders and hung down to around the middle of her back. He noticed she had something around her neck, but he could not make it out from that distance. He thought about why she happened to be there and figured she might have been a new employee taking the standard, hands-on tour from the administration. In any event, he began to fantasize about her, there in the hallway of the maternity ward with his wife no more than twenty to thirty feet away from him.

As he yearned to become lost within her eyes, he pondered about what colour they were behind those full lashes. He wanted to take her in his arms and caress the small of her back with one hand while he stroked her soot black hair with the other. Such enchantment added to her beauty. He started to conceive situations in which he was a holy knight or prince or some other noble persona/warrior, saving her from some horrid overlord, family member, or beast. He dreamed of conquering nations and dragons to obtain her for even the smallest possibility of embracing her luscious, welcoming lips. He wished he hadn't married the woman he impregnated, but, because they were both Catholic, it seemed only natural to go about that way. Regardless of this fact, he fantasized about all the ways he could approach her and engage her in conversation without seeming like a low criminal because he had abandoned his wife.

Mr. O'Brian prayed to anything he could conceive of during these time-stopping moments. God, Satan, Buddha, Aphrodite, Freyja, and more were all invoked for the smallest chance she would turn her head, even if just for a second, and notice him sitting there. He tried to make himself look miserable or distraught, but, if she had looked at him, she would have noticed it was simply nothing more than bad acting. He suddenly became upset with himself.

"Damn it," he whispered. He now wished he had brought the video camera to record his son's birth instead of leaving it accidentally on purpose at his house in the ensuing panic his wife put him through as her water broke.

"To hell with the whole delivery and new life is so beautiful that it must be caught on film," he thought. He did not wish to relive the death of his former existence by watching life. Instead, the video camera could have served a better purpose for him, being able to capture her presence on tape so he could watch it in secret. He did not care what his wife would have said when he told her he had lost the tape, as he thought that birth was a rather mundane and overplayed miracle.

As he continued to sit there, entranced by her beauty, he had a thought that had never crossed his mind before. He thought about murdering his wife and framing it as a postpartum depression suicide. It was the only way out after all. He could not get a divorce and be married in a church ceremony once again because of the whole thing about not parting 'til death. He thought about it a little longer, scratched some parts of this idea, and expanded on what he had left.

Maybe instead of a suicide, which the child's mother would have performed on herself after killing their child anyway, he could have caught her in the act and murder her in order to save his now most precious child. During this rescue of his son, he would have, of course, wounded himself in the process. The wound would be big enough to attain some sympathy, but small enough so it would not affect anything of vital importance. After murdering and framing his wife, he figured he'd drive as a reckless maniac and check back into this specific hospital, even though it was out of his way, seeing how this hospital's specialty was its children's ward. He would make the extra distance to ensure the survival of his son. Such was the justification in his own mind. He was certain that, after such an ordeal, word of mouth from the other wards of his heroic deed would have trickled down through the grapevine. Maybe he'd finally be able to have his conversation with her when he came to check on his son. She knew it would be him because of his battle wounds wrapped in plaster or gauze. This was sound reasoning to him and a safe, quick way into her heart.

Suddenly, a tap on his left shoulder startled Mr. O'Brian out of his enchantment and brought him back to his ever-worsening reality. He looked up. It was Evelyn.

"Mr. O'Brian, someone here wants to meet you."

He stood up and entered the delivery room with his head still somewhat hanging. He closed the door behind him. Evelyn thought nothing of it other than how he was still suffering from the humiliation he had received a few moments earlier, not because he never saw the young woman's eyes. She started to make her way back into the delivery room. Before she could, the lanky, middle-aged woman with the clipboard called over to her.

"Yes, Ms. Fraystl?" Evelyn responded.

Ms. Fraystl and the young woman stopped in front of her.

"I would like to introduce you to the new nurse, Lily."

Lily outstretched her right arm to shake Evelyn's hand.

"Hi, I'm Evelyn," she said cheerfully as she shook Lily's hand.

Ms. Fraystl pushed the clipboard up to her chest with her left arm. Her right arm motioned toward Evelyn as she looked at Lily.

"Evelyn has been with us for a couple years now on this ward. She came right off university, which means you two are probably around the same age as each other."

Evelyn put her left hand behind her. "The internship essentially provided the job for me."

"You're being too modest," said Ms. Fraystl. "You know we would have hired you even if you had interned elsewhere. You came highly recommended, just like Lily here."

Evelyn turned her head toward Lily. "So you're just out of school yourself?"

Lily turned her right hand to the side, exposing her palm. "Actually no. I graduated in what seems to be an eternity ago."

"I know what you mean. It's a completely different world than it was before all of this." Evelyn used her arms to emphasize her surroundings.

Lily grinned.

"Evelyn, can you do me a favour?"

"Sure, Ms. Fraystl. What is it?"

"I have a ton of calls and orders to place." She stopped pressing the clipboard up against herself and looked down at it. "Someone miscounted our supplies so I've fallen behind. Can you finish showing Lily around here for me? She starts on Monday."

Evelyn told Ms. Fraystl that she would be happy to do so.

"Thank you, Evelyn. I'll see the two of you on Monday."

She turned around and headed back toward the administrative office. The two girls looked at each other and started walking closely down the mock granite-coloured hallways. Evelyn resumed the tour for Lily that Ms. Fraystl had already started.

"Well, there really isn't much left to show you on the tour except for the nursery and your locker so I guess you can tell me about yourself as we head on over to the nursery."

Lily placed her arms behind her back as she walked. "There's not much to tell except that I love children in a nonpedophile way. That's why I took this job. I just can't get enough of them."

Evelyn looked to her right and Lily.

"I used to be a daycare supervisor and teacher for toddlers some years back and an orphanage director before that."

They turned left and down a corridor, walking past open doors and mostly empty rooms.

"How many children did you care for? In the daycare, I mean."

Lily looked to her left toward Evelyn. "Fifteen or so on average. Some days more, some days less. You know how it is. You have the regulars, and then you have the drop-ins."

Evelyn looked forward. Her eyebrows lifted. "Wow. Fifteen on average. It's not that bad here. We don't really deal with toddlers on this ward though. We're essentially strictly newborns. Toddlers through age thirteen are on the floor above us. Kind of makes us lucky as we don't have to run after them all the time."

Lily's head now was facing forward. She smiled with closed lips. "Those little ones can really run you ragged. So fancy and carefree until they stumble into something and start to cry. At least if they do that here, they're already in a hospital."

Evelyn laughed. "True."

The two came around yet another corner of the hallway. Evelyn stopped walking. She pointed over to a glass window that was used as a separation for the newborns. "Here's the nursery."

Lily stepped forward and placed her right hand, palm open flush onto the glass. She looked at the few children that were laying in basinets inside the nursery. She closed her eyes. Evelyn watched. After a brief moment, Lily opened her eyes and removed her palm from the glass. Evelyn walked up next to Lily and stood to her right. As they both peered into the nursery, Evelyn was about to ask Lily if she had any children of her own. Before she could, a plump nurse walked into the nursery from the side opposite the glass. She was carrying something small and pink wrapped in a light blue blanket.

"Ah!" Lily smiled. "A new edition."

"That's the O'Brian baby. I finished helping the delivery of their son just before I met you." Evelyn waved to the nurse behind the glass, who waved back. "Which brings me to telling you the best part about this job. The stories you hear from some of the women."

Lily quickly knew where Evelyn was headed. "You mean those speeches that go about the likes of 'You did this to me!' or 'This is so wonderful! I love you, honey?'"

Evelyn snapped her left fingers. "Bingo. But every now and again, we get to hear some interesting variations. Take the O'Brian baby that Tamara just placed down. During that delivery, Mrs. O'Brian embarrassed her husband so much that he had to leave the room."

"What did she say exactly?"

"She basically let everyone know that he had a small penis and he was so inept that he could never give her an orgasm." Evelyn described the humorous scene from the delivery room.

Lily laughed at how funny Mrs. O'Brian's comment toward her son pleasing a woman more than her husband could. "That's hilarious, even if it's very Oedipal in nature."

Evelyn giggled at Lily's comment. She placed her arm around her, as a sister would.

"Come. Let's get you to your locker. It's not too far from here."

The two left the separating wall and walked down the rest of the hallway. Evelyn had completely forgotten about asking Lily if she had any children. She was just happy to have someone around her age on the ward again. It was not like she hated the other nurses, but they were older and had families of their own. They came from a different generation, an older generation. It was hard for her to relate herself to those who had much more experience. She was happy with this new sister-in-trade and just went with the flow of the conversation until they made their way to the locker room.

"Take your pick of locker, Lily. Just find one that isn't marked. That shouldn't be a problem, considering there are more lockers than nurses. Just remember to bring a lock on Monday, and you're set."

Evelyn began to strip down to her undergarments while Lily was wandering around the locker room. She came around the corner from behind a set of lockers and observed Evelyn's slim figure. Lily stood there with her right foot crossed and placed slightly in front of her left. She noticed Evelyn's strawberry blonde hair was now down, and she was in a pair of jeans and a white bra.

"Nice figure, Evelyn. It's too bad that the nurse's smock hides it. Remind me not to wear mine outside the hospital."

"Yeah." Evelyn laughed. "They're not too terribly forgiving, but, with your figure, even with these hideous smocks, you shouldn't be too bad off, at least not as bad off as me."

Evelyn pulled a tight black sweater over her head. She grabbed her purse out from her locker, put it over her left shoulder, and moved to Lily after closing the locker door. "There's one place left on the tour."

Lily was intrigued. The two left the locker room and began making their way over to the elevator while chitchatting about the layout and design of the hospital.

"I noticed there were a couple guards near the nurses' station when I walked in," Lily said.

"Those two are Bruce and Ryan. They're harmless really. We have them mostly because it would be too expensive to have an interconnecting security system installed in this old building."

"So the security system is based off each floor?"

Evelyn nodded. "That's right. It's basic yet effective. I wish we did have a modern system though."

"Still, you can't argue with what works."

Evelyn waved to Bruce and Ryan as they passed by them as they continued to the elevators. Once there, Lily pressed the down button to summon it. As they were waiting, Lily looked to her left and noticed the double doors to the stairwell. The handles were rectangular pull bows with a lock lever one could push down with their thumb as they pulled the door toward themselves to open it.

The elevator made its standard pinging noise, and the doors opened. They walked in, and Evelyn pressed the button for the main floor. The elevator closed its doors and started to descend. They were continuing with their idle chitchat when the elevator stopped on the fourth floor. The doors opened, and Evelyn flinched. Lily noticed this, but said nothing. Evelyn hated the fourth floor. It was the long-term care ward for the hospital, a place where once admitted, the only way to leave is through death. If Lily had known that both of Evelyn's parents had passed away on this ward, she may have found it strange that Evelyn worked at this particular hospital. A weeping elderly couple with what appeared to be their two granddaughters and single grandson stepped inside the stopped elevator. The doors closed, and the elevator's descent continued. All inside the elevator was quiet now, except for the echoing sounds from tears staining the floor. The ride finished soon thereafter, and the inhabitants silently left the small box. The family of five walked forward to the reception desk found in the middle of the main floor and turned to leave the hospital from the entrance's sliding doors. Lily and Evelyn continued passed the circular reception desk and down a ramp that led to a hall. They stepped inside.

"This is the cafeteria," Evelyn told her.

Lily took a look around the mostly white room. She noticed a long lineup where the food was being served. There were cafeteria tables, some rectangular with many attached benches for seats as well as the occasional circular one. High-standing bistro tables with two chairs accompanying each were also placed around the hall.

Lily looked over to Evelyn. "Is the food here as good as it is in every other cafeteria?"

Evelyn laughed. "I actually think worse, but there's more to this cafeteria than most others." Evelyn explained that the cafeteria was a calling ground of sorts for the entire hospital staff. She was informed that all the doctors and nurses per floor had their own break periods and each employee had their own specific break time.

"Your breaks will vary depending on how busy we are. That reminds me. You'll be getting a pager on Monday as well. It's mostly there for emergency situations, so, even if you are on break, you can run up the stairs as the elevator isn't so good in an emergency on a busy day anyway."

A pair of hands came down over Evelyn's face. "Guess who, honey?"

"I'm thinking that it's Jesse," she said. "You know him, right? My former boyfriend that I had to let go because he wouldn't stop being a goof and blinding me from behind."

Jesse quickly took his hands off of her face. Evelyn turned around and faced him. He had black, chin-length hair and chestnut-coloured eyes. He looked fairly athletic, especially in his legs. They closed their eyes and kissed a lover's kiss.

"You're off later than you should have been, Evey."

Evelyn sighed. "Another last-second birth … as usual."

Jesse noticed Lily standing there beside Evelyn. "So, Evey, are you going to introduce me to your friend or what?"

"Where are my manners? Jesse, this is Lily. She's a new nurse who will be working with me come Monday."

Jesse stuck out his hand. Lily shook it. He gazed past her full lashes and into her hazel eyes. He noticed a hint of emerald green within them.

"Lily, this is Jesse, my boyfriend."

"Also a nurse?"

"Why does no one ever ask doctor?" Jesse replied.

Evelyn rolled her bright blue eyes.

Jesse laughed playfully. "Yeah, I'm a nurse. I work on the floor above you two, but I like to think of it more than just being a nurse."

"And that would be?" Lily asked.

"Because of how often I chase the children who escape their beds around the floor, I like to think that it's training for the Olympics in any sort of sprinting event. It must be working," he enthusiastically declared. "Just look at these legs of mine."

Evelyn rolled her bright blue eyes once more. "Just ignore him, Lily. He's quite the smartass at times."

He looked over to Evelyn. "I thought that was part of my charm?" He leaned in to kiss her, but she moved away and turned.

"There you go, flattering yourself again."

Jesse placed his right hand on the back of his head and rubbed his hair. "One has to go with his strong points."

Evelyn smiled, but did not turn around. Nevertheless, Jesse knew he had made her smile.

"Lily, Jesse and I were going for dinner. Would you like to join us?"

"That's all right, Evelyn. You've done more than enough for me already. Besides, I don't wish to impose on the two of you."

Evelyn put up her hands and shook them. "It's no imposition. We're going to be working together a lot anyway."

Jesse interjected. "You'll have to excuse Evey here. She's an only child, and she has always wanted a sister around her age."

"I understand how she feels. I'm an only child as well."

Evelyn's face lit up. "Well, then you're definitely coming with us." She turned to Jesse. "We insist, don't we, Jesse?"

He nodded his head in agreement. "Definitely."

Lily made it seem as if she were giving it some deep thought, even though she immediately had an answer. "All right then. Since you two insist and all. Sounds like fun."

"Great!" Evelyn said with much glee.

The three took their leave of the mess hall and walked toward the exit that led to the back parking lot.

As they were walking, Lily remembered something and stopped. "I just remembered something. I need to quickly run back up and talk to Ms. Fraystl for a second."

"Everything all right?" Evelyn asked.

"Yes. It's just a business thing, nothing to worry about. Is it all right if I meet you two there?"

"Sure," said Jesse.

"Outstanding. Where's the restaurant?"

"It's the Ivy on Cygnus Street," Evelyn stated. "Do you know it?"

Lily shook her head no. "Not really, but don't worry about me. I'll be able to find it. I'll see you two in a few."

Lily waved good-bye and headed to the elevator while Jesse and Evelyn went to their car. In the parking lot, Jesse noticed a car he had never seen parked in the employee spaces before, a burgundy 1950 Jaguar XK120 roadster. He assumed it belonged to Lily, as she was the only new hire he knew about. Jesse couldn't take his eyes off it until he finally walked straight into a van. Evelyn looked at him. He shook his head to ease away the dizziness.

"Wish I could make you turn your head like that," Evelyn taunted.

Jesse looked for words.

"I'm joking, hun," Evelyn laughed playfully. "No need to go completely silent."

Jesse put his right hand on the backside of his head as he smiled. "I know."

He tried to think of a good bantering comeback, but he was still dazed from the van. When they finally arrived at their humble little car, Jesse opened the passenger's side door for Evelyn before jumping into the driver's seat. He started up the engine, and off they went to the restaurant.

Two

"Table for three?"

"Yes, please," Evelyn said to the hostess. "A booth, if possible."

"I think that can be arranged."

The hostess took three menus and led the diners to their seats. The restaurant was dimly lit from the sconces lining the walls and support columns. It was spacious enough, and the patrons were far enough away from each other so their voices did not combine into one overwhelming plethora of noise. It had an atmosphere that accompanies proper dining, not one where you eat and then quickly rush out. Eventually, they reached a booth that was next to a large picture window. They had a view of a small valley. A cool breeze was blowing the leaves on a beautiful autumn day as the sun was beginning to set. Evelyn and Jesse sat next to each other while Lily sat opposite them.

"Your server will be with you momentarily." The hostess walked away and back to her station.

The three opened their menus. Lily smiled. "How's the food here?"

"Only the best in town," Evelyn cheerfully answered.

"Is that so?" Lily's eyes were surveying the menu in front of her. "I really don't have anything to compare it to though."

Evelyn looked up from her menu. "What do you mean?"

"I've never been to a restaurant in this town before Evelyn. I've only lived here for a little over a week."

Evelyn placed down her menu. "Really?"

Lily folded and placed her menu down in front of her. "Yes, I left everyone behind to come here and take this job."

"Sorry to hear that," Evelyn said.

Lily smirked. "Don't be. Sometimes, one just has to do what one has to do."

"Do you need any help moving anything in? Jesse and I are available."

Jesse rolled his eyes. "There you go, offering my help again." He kept his eyes on his menu.

Evelyn ignored him and asked her if she needed any help again.

"I've already moved in everything that has to be moved in. There is no need to worry, you two."

"Where are you living?" Evelyn asked her.

"Three Seven Sentential Crescent Court."

Jesse suddenly became interested in the conversation after he heard the address. Crescent Court was not exactly situated in town. It was high-end, and most of the estates were usually passed down through the generations of blue bloods. If a house ever became available, one would need to have a lot of money in order to afford it.

He lowered his menu. "How could you afford the house and classic roadster? Is someone paying your way?"

Lily shook her head from side to side.

"Then how can you afford to pay that mortgage?"

"I paid in cash and bought it outright. There's no mortgage."

Jesse was confused. "How?"

"Simple. It's my money. It's all in my name and my name alone."

He leaned forward with astonishment. "Jesus Christ! How'd you manage that?" Jokingly, he asked, "Did you rob a bank or something?"

Lily smirked. "I haven't robbed a bank, but I have made some smart investments over the years."

Jesse leaned back. "You must have if you're living there. Are you sure everything has been moved in? I mean I can carry, hold, and restrain quite a bit of weight. Just ask the kids on my ward."

Lily smirked at Jesse's obvious attempt. "Yes, everything's been moved in, although there are still a few things I have to move around and take out of boxes. It may take a while, but, when I do become settled, I'll be more than happy to play your host."

Jesse's eyes lit up. He was about to say something, but stopped due to the appearance of a slender, auburn-haired young man who was standing at the end side of the table.

"Hello," he said. "My name is Seth, and I'll be your server for this evening."

Lily looked up at Seth and stopped him before he was able to continue. "Seth, eh? I'm assuming you come from some Christian background. Or are your parents Pharaohs who decided to spell Set with an h?"

Seth turned his head to Lily. "Catholic actually, and, I must say, I'm impressed. Most people don't pick up on the name. They really only know, or rather care, about the other two sons: Cain and Abel. Especially Cain."

Lily grinned with closed lips. "I've never cared for that goody-goody Abel. Cain is quite the character though."

"Exactly my point," Seth said. "I'm just a replacement."

"It's quite interesting that you happen to be our server for the evening, Seth."

"And why would that be, miss?" Seth joyfully asked. "I'm sorry. I didn't catch your name."

"It's Lily."

"As in the beautiful flower?"

"Not exactly, Seth."

Seth was straightforward. "How many men have used that line on you?"

Lily kept a smile, but did not blush. "Too many times to count."

She explained that she did like hearing it from time to time, but there were many different types of lilies, all of which symbolize different things.

"Most men don't think of that when they hit on me. To them, the name is just the generic flower grouping." She said she may not even be a true 'Lily' after all. "Perhaps I'm a Lillian, a Lilah, or even a Susan who just prefers to go by Lily."

Seth tilted his head slightly to the right. "But isn't Lillian Latin for Lily anyhow? Susan, isn't that the English form of Susanna, the Greek form of the Hebrew Shoshannah, as in the flower, be it a lily or a rose in the Song of Songs?" He took a moment to think. "Lilah, that's a tricky one. According to the French and German spellings, without the H at the end, it is a lilac, another flower, and short form for Delilah in Arabic. If the h at the end of the name is present, then it's a form of Delilah from the Hebrew."

The emerald in her eyes flickered. "Clever boy. How have you come to know of such things off the top of your head? Most people don't care anymore."

Seth opened his left hand and placed it on his hip. "It's somewhat of a hobby of mine. Names and origins have always interested me."

Lily scanned him as she smirked on the right side of her face. "Since you've come to know so much about names, allow me to formally introduce myself."

Seth became intrigued.

"My full name is Lillian Clement. Do what you will with that, but I have just one small favour."

"And what would that be?"

"Don't call me Lillian."

Seth smiled. While he was doing so, he noticed the ornamental cross hanging around her neck. "That's a lovely cross, Lily."

Lily grabbed the cross with her right thumb and index finger. She started to play with it flirtatiously. "This old thing? It's nothing much. Just a pure silver, Knights Templars cross fashioned from a Cross Fitchy. I'd rather the Jerusalem Cross, but having those four little crosses join on a necklace is troublesome."

"No doubt," said Seth. "I remember the pictures of your cross on shields from history class. On a crusade now, are we?"

Lily leaned in closer to Seth and the table's edge. "Aren't we all?"

"Granted." He decided to bring the conversation back to its start. "I feel as if I could talk to you on such matters all day, but I'm curious. Why is it interesting that I happen to be your server tonight?"

Lily turned her right hand to the side to get Seth to turn his head to Evelyn. "You see this woman sitting across from me?"

"Yes."

"Her name is Evelyn."

Seth raised an eyebrow. "Now that is interesting."

Lily and Seth shared a chuckle while Jesse and Evelyn stared blankly at each other.

"Evelyn, sweetie." Lily said. "Not that I am going to go into detail on your name, as it can have its roots and variations in French, German, and Latin, but drop the Lyn and you have Eve, as in Adam and Eve, as in the mother of Cain, Abel, and then Seth."

Evelyn shook her head from side to side quickly as if she were coming out of a daze. "Oh yeah! Sorry, religion is sort of over my head at times, as I've forgotten most of it over my years."

Seth modestly smiled. "No worry there, Mum. Now before I forget or we get off topic again, today's special is a tuna steak with lemon and olive oil over a bed of roasted potatoes and other vegetables. Now, may I get you anything to drink while you decide on your meal?"

"I'll have a glass of Merlot," Lily said. "On second thought, bring a forty-ounce bottle instead."

"That's quite a bit," Evelyn stated.

"It's for the table. Think of it as my treat for you two showing me around."

"Thank you," Evelyn said. "Just so you know though, some of us here aren't exactly wine drinkers." Evelyn put up her closed menu to the side of her face to hide her emphasis of Jesse while she pointed in his direction with her free hand.

"Speaking of which," Jesse said. "I'll have an ale."

Seth slightly turned his head closer to the table's edge. "And anything for you, Mum?"

"Sure. Why not? A glass of Sauvignon blanc would be lovely."

"Very good. I'll be back with your drinks shortly."

After Seth left, Lily crossed her arms over her menu and looked across the table as she slightly leaned forward. "I noticed the looks on your faces while Seth and I were talking. You two aren't overly religious, are you?"

They both shook their heads no. Jesse answered for the both of them. "I'm an evolutionist, and she's more of the classical period, at least in terms of stories."

Lily placed her right thumb and index finger near the bottom of her chin. "I can see Evelyn's point of view. There's at least some basis of faith in those stories, but I don't understand you people, Jesse." She removed her hand from under her chin. "I mean, I can see your point of view clearly through the microscope, but still."

"You don't think we can't have faith in evolution and science as a society?"

Seth returned with the drinks a few moments later and placed them down on the table as Lily and Jesse conversed. He was ready to see if they had made up their minds and take their order, but he wanted to hear the conversation so he did not interrupt.

"I just think it's foolish to think purely in scientific and evolutionist terms, but that's where the world is heading. To take a page from the classics index, the Greeks discovered many ways to explain natural elements that we still use as a basis. They put their gods separate from science, but didn't discount them while they were making their discoveries. If they did, then Rome wouldn't have adopted and preserved the myths. They would have died when they took over."

Jesse leaned in closer across the table. "Well, then how do you explain evolution?"

"God didn't create the world in seven days. He didn't create mankind in his image or anything else of the sort. That's just the works from the poets of yesteryear. He allowed for evolution in beings that he formerly created, such as dinosaurs into birds, to take over for him, letting nature take its course. You should know about that. Anyhow, after scraping a few projects via worldwide disasters, the primate was created and survived. He liked the form so he began fine-tuning it, tweaking it over the years in some sort of cosmic workshop. After every new form was created, they were given life. This is where all the gorillas, Neanderthals, and Homo and pre-homo species classified by science come from. This is also why human beings share close DNA and primitive traits with these creatures."

Jesse intently hung on to her every word.

"As the countless years of perfection went by, not all of these creatures survived the environment in which they found themselves in. Eventually, after many tests, he finally perfected the image inside his head and created a paradise for them to live in, separate from the world that was already going on around them. He loved them so much that he even decided to grant them immortality, but he overlooked one thing in his glory."

Evelyn asked her what this was.

Lily turned her head to her. "We weren't perfect."

Jesse scoffed. "I could have told you that one."

Lily turned her head back to Jesse. "Yes, but do you know the reason why?"

Jesse refrained from scratching his head as he had no response.

"He could never root out that primitive influence from which the original design was based upon. The namesake of she who is sitting next to you and her husband got themselves into trouble. As an angry first-time parent, as he made himself known to them, expelled those two fools from that garden. Now regardless of this fact, science and religion are both correct. Creationism evolved."

Jesse was rendered completely silent. He, and for that matter most everyone else, could never conceive such a radical idea that seemed very plausible, even if one had to make the leap to get there. Seth noticed the look on Jesse's face and took this free time to ask if they had decided. Lily ordered a garden salad and roasted lamb with rice and vegetables. Evelyn chose the Greek salad with pasta primavera, and Jesse ordered the bruschetta and a New York steak well done with a baked potato and sour cream. With their orders placed, the triumvirate of diners handed Seth their menus. As he was walking away, Jesse started in on the Bible to Lily as she was pouring some of the Merlot into her glass. After she finished pouring her drink and Jesse stopped talking, she answered his small rant of the topic.

"Jesse, men wrote those Scriptures. They just interpreted everything their own way. Of course they embellished the human race as a divine form. Remember what I said about not being created in his image?" She lifted her glass and took a sip of her wine.

"So just for the record, you admit yourself that the Bible is screwy." Jesse placed his right hand around his tall glass of ale.

"Well of course, I do," she admitted openly. "The Scriptures can be very ambiguous. You would be surprised how inaccurate the authors were in regards to those events as they mostly wrote for effect. One must remember that there are many different interpretations and expansions of it."

Evelyn had a drink of her wine as she listened to Lily.

"The Torah and the rest of the Tanakh, Qur'an, New Testament of the Christian lexicon, and not to mention all of those other translations that are floating around out there. With each new interpretation, things change, sometimes subtle but still. People like to interpret these words according to their own lives, culture, or state of the world."

"That being your case then," Evelyn said, "is there any particular version you prefer?"

Lily looked into her red wine and then across the table at her inquisitive friend. "I tend toward the older texts. You two would recognize some of it as the Old Testament."

"And why is that?" Jesse asked.

"I prefer these because the newer Testaments make God out to be all lovey-dovey and noble. In the older texts, he had a noticeable, active role on this planet. Now we have this dime-store statement of 'mysterious ways in which he works,' and it irritates me to no end."

The couple sort of glanced at her.

The emerald sparkled. "Look, you can't take everything found in the Scriptures so seriously because, if you do, you become rigid. Protests, uprisings, wars, and more become suddenly justified because of that. I'm not a textbook believer."

"What do you mean by textbook believer?" Evelyn asked.

Lily decided an example would be the best way to answer. "Take the flood in the King James translation of Genesis because King James is used as the canonical Bible nowadays. Chapter 7:4 mentions the forty days and forty nights of rain. Chapter 7:24 states one hundred and fifty days the waters prevailed upon the earth or something like that."

Jesse moved his right hand clockwise quickly a few times. "Your point?"

Lily slightly shifted her head to him. "The entire thing was somewhere around one hundred and ninety days. Noah opening his window to check the status of the known world at that time by releasing the birds is just a quick jump back to make it sound inspirational and becoming between days forty and one hundred ninety."

"Come now," Jesse leaned forward toward Lily. "You really think that it was somewhere around one hundred and ninety days?"

"I don't think it. I know it," she said with conviction.

"And how exactly is that? You yourself stated the ambiguities."

Lily shook her head in agreement. "That I did. Despite the Bible's ambiguities, it's up to the individual to make the jump, the connections. The Scriptures are not supposed to be static. People read into things too literally nowadays. That's why there has been a disappearance of faith in society. Mankind has lost something pivotal along the way, and it's such a shame."

Jesse leaned back in the booth.

Evelyn removed her hand from her wine glass. "So you go to church every Sunday, memorize passages, and other things like that?"

Lily quickly shook her left hand back and forth just above the table. "No, I don't. I enjoy my pleasures. I don't need to go to church in order to be a good or righteous person."

Evelyn tilted her head slightly to her right in curiosity.

"I don't pray or offer a toast to my meal before I eat. I take immense pleasure in every salacious situation I find myself in. I ask you. Do you see a husband or even a boyfriend sitting here next to me? I like money and what I can get in exchange for it. I have much pride in my tasks and what I do, although I sometimes neglect my duties and just lounge about. At times, I have become envious of others. I do have a temper. Although it doesn't go off too often, may God have mercy on the souls of those who get in the way of my wrath."

Jesse had a drink of his ale.

"People assume they have to go to church, and that makes the sermon seem like a chore to them. Those who assume they have to go become more hypocritical than anything else. These people are even worse than those that just go in times of need. It doesn't help the children who are forced to accompany their parents to these sermons either. Sometimes, because of this very act, they rebel against it when they start developing an ideology and image for themselves."

Jesse asked her why she thought this.

"Besides how people can't think for themselves and secretly prefer to be told how to live their lives?"

He nodded at her.

"Religion is about influence. Influence, not faith, is what this world is truly about."

Evelyn had to know. "What exactly do you mean by that?"

Lily looked at her. "Take a look around at all the trends people take to." She moved her arms to indicate all surroundings. "A lot of this world wanders around and never thinks outside of the box. People aren't snowflakes, as most tend to believe. They know not what they do." She reached for her wine glass. "It's all about influence. Always has been, always will be." She drank her wine.

"I see your point, but enough of these theoretical debates." Evelyn looked over at Jesse. "He's too stubborn to give up when he knows he's beat, so this will carry on all night long." She turned her attention back to Lily. "Anyway, what do you think of our waiter?"

"He's cute. His looks remind me of someone I once knew, but I can't quite place my finger on whom."

"That aside," Evelyn said, "you two seem to have such a good connection already. You should go for it."

Jesse sighed. "There you go, playing matchmaker again."

Evelyn ignored him. "Are you actually considering it?"

"I'm not so sure if now is the appropriate time for such an endeavour," she modestly replied. "It's tricky for me to be in a relationship with anyone anyhow."

"And why is that?" Evelyn asked as her curiosity was beginning to get the better of her.

"I seem to have a strange effect on certain types of men."

Jesse and Evelyn looked at her inquisitively. Jesse was going to ask her, but he knew Evelyn would do it for him.

"I mean, these types become infatuated with me in a crazy type way. Sometimes, they make it easily apparent, and they have the typical schoolboy crush on me. Some others, though, tend to let it seep and fester. That's why I had to leave my last job as the daycare supervisor. The headmistress' husband became so enamoured with my presence there that he made a fervent pass at me. Because his feelings festered, he ran amok with his semiautomatic rifle when I told him I wasn't interested even in the slightest. I never did attend those funerals after that event."

"Christ! What happened?" Jesse asked.

Lily took a sip of her wine. "I took care of it. That's all."

Evelyn and Jesse looked blankly at each other.

"Oh, come now." Lily laughed lightheartedly. "All I did was protect the children and call the police. It's not like I killed him. That was the work of the police during the standoff."

Jesse and Evelyn breathed a sigh of relief.

"It's not too often that this happens though. I believe it's something on the genetic level, something that a forefather in their lineage passed down to them."

She looked out the window and noticed a tree branch bending in the gentle breeze. She turned back toward Jesse and Evelyn. "Our good boy, Seth, here seems to have his blood diluted enough so he would be a good candidate, but I'd like to settle a little bit before I go jumping on the first bipedal thing with a pulse."

Evelyn nodded. "That makes sense."

"Perhaps we should come back in about a month's time and see what—"

Evelyn cut off Lily by placing an index finger up to her nose and over her mouth. She noticed Seth was making his way back to the table with the appetizers. He placed the appetizers down on the table and left to take another order. Lily placed her napkin in her lap.

"So," Evelyn said, "now that you've watched him walk away and seen the full frame, change your mind about him?"

Jesse sighed. "Just leave her alone already. He's probably not her type. Considering how refined she is, Seth probably isn't old enough for her anyway."

"And just what are you implying there, Jesse?" Lily asked. "Are you implying that I have father issues, seeing how he's not old enough?"

Jesse gave Lily a well-do-you look while Evelyn snagged one of the small pieces of Italian bread from his plate.

"I don't seek out father figures for physical or mental comfort."

Evelyn put the newly bitten piece of Italian bread down and placed it next to her salad before speaking. "You mentioned you were also an only child. How's your relationship with the family?"

"My father and I are estranged. We're still on good terms though. I still talk to him from time to time." Lily forked herself some salad from her plate.

"What happened to cause the rift?" Evelyn asked.

"It's long and complicated." Lily wiped the corners of her mouth with her napkin. "I'll give you the short, simplified version of it."

Evelyn started her salad as Jesse picked up a small piece of Italian bread.

"He picked a suitor for me. He wasn't even a good suitor at that, but my father treated him like a son he never had. When I had enough of him and left home, Father helped him find someone to replace me."

Evelyn was shocked.

"The suitor was bloody contemptible. He always wanted to be on top of things. He complained because I saw us as equals and wouldn't let him have his day. I guess that's just my independence talking, but still. He pissed and moaned about it to Father. I had enough of him, so I left." Lily took a drink of her wine and then placed it back on the table in front of her. "After I left him, he bawled and became depressed at his newfound loneliness. I guess Father felt sorry for the boor, so he helped him find a replacement after I conveyed my intent to not return. In any event, I know my father cared more for me than he let on, even if he will never admit to it. He is stubborn that way."

"And how exactly do you know this?" Jesse asked.

Evelyn took her wine glass in hand.

"The woman he replaced me with was very subpar. She caused my former spouse more problems than anything else in the long run. Despite all that happened, I don't think he ever got over me. It's funny how things work out sometimes."

Evelyn had to know Lily's reasoning. "How can you still not be angry with your father? He picked a man for you, for Christ's sakes!"

Jesse reached for his ale.

Lily sombrely looked down at the table. "That was a long time ago."

"It couldn't have been that long ago. I mean, you're our age. It's just—"

Jesse interrupted his now-stuttering girlfriend. "Fathers sometimes think they know what's best for their daughters, Evey. Your father and I got along great, but, deep down, he knew what was going on between you and me, especially after we moved in together without being married, so there was always that weird, unspoken rift between us."

"I suppose you're right." She laughed and slowly shook her head from side to side. "Fathers and their daughters."

Lily timidly smirked as she brought the wine glass up to her mouth.

"How's the relationship with your mother?" Evelyn asked as Jesse took a swig of his ale.

Lily placed the wine back down before her. "I never came to know her. She was never around. I can't even remember what she looks like. As far as I'm concerned, I have no mother." Lily wiped the sides of her mouth with her napkin.

"Aunts and uncles?"

"Many, on my father's side. They were usually off helping Father in his work though. It's sort of a family-owned business." Lily noticed the look on Evelyn's face. "Don't feel sorry for me, Evelyn. I have my own life, and

I'm happy with it. Perhaps someday I'll be running the business anyhow or even one of my own. Let's just see how things play out."

"You'll have to excuse her, Lily." Jesse placed his glass next to his plate. "She's had a good upbringing, growing up with a close-knit family in an open house with no sudden deaths or tragedies. Whenever she hears something upsetting in a person's background, she just feels sorry for them. It's quite cute in a weird way." Jesse patted her on the head.

Evelyn playfully gave Jesse a push.

"So how long have you two been an item?"

"It seems like forever and a day."

Evelyn gave Jesse a spirited look for his response. "Shush, you. It's only been about five years."

"Really? Five years? Congratulations. Although usually after such a period, the woman is wearing a ring on her finger."

Evelyn did not move her head, but her bright blue eyes moved slightly to her right. "That's because Jesse here doesn't believe in marriage."

"Here we go with this again." Jesse looked over the table. "Lily, do you believe in marriage?"

"Well, that's not fair," Evelyn said defensively. "Her father picked a suitor for her. Of course she's going to take your side."

Jesse grinned. "That's kind of the point."

"This may surprise you," Lily interrupted, "but I do believe in marriage, both kinds. I don't necessarily believe in the people who get married though, as now it seems to just be something of a fashion statement. The concept behind marriage has changed over the years."

"Just what do you mean by both kinds?" Evelyn questioned.

"Marriages based on love are still relatively new, and one would figure that they would be highly successful. On the other hand, arranged marriages have a lower divorce rate than those who wed for love. Granted, my arranged wedlock didn't work out, but that's beside the point."

Jesse pushed his plate away from him into the center of the table.

"But you would marry for love? Wouldn't you?" Evelyn asked her.

"I have."

She gave Lily a ponderous look. "Just exactly how many times have you been married?"

"Twice," she modestly answered.

Evelyn looked at Lily's left hand. "But there's no ring on that finger of yours. How'd it end?"

"Actually, it didn't. I guess you could say I'm still technically married."

"Technically?" Evelyn said with a confused tone. "How's that work?"

"We didn't separate, get a divorce, or anything of that sort. I lost track of him over the years. I'm in a type of marriage limbo so I don't wear a ring."

Evelyn asked her if she missed him.

Lily sombrely looked at her now-empty plate. She reached for her wine glass. "Deeply. I remember the last time I saw him. It feels as if it were yesterday." She stared at the wine sitting peacefully in her glass. She had a drink and placed the glass back on the table. She placed her right thumb on the front of the stem while her index, middle, and ring fingers held the stem's back. "We were lying in bed next to each other. He was caressing my neck with his index and middle fingers while whispering sweet nothings in my ear as his other arm was draped around me." She smiled almost blushingly at this memory. "I know. I know. How romantically stereotypical, but it was still sweet." Her eyes came back to their proper level. "As he continued to work his way down my figure line, I turned around and faced him. We gazed into each other's eyes, and we silently asked each other what we were going to do."

Evelyn placed her salad fork across the middle of her plate. "Going to do about what?"

"You know that feeling you get when something is up in the air and just doesn't feel right?" Evelyn nodded. "Well, we both knew something like that was coming our way, but we just didn't know when or what it would be, so we had this long conversation about what we were going to do and how we would prepare for it. After we finished talking, he rose up and out of bed, dressed himself, and left. That was that. There was no good-bye or other formal end to the marriage. We vowed to each other that, if we ever came across each other's paths at any point in time again, after whatever immanent disaster that was ahead in our lives passed, we would get back together. That's why we never ended the marriage."

Evelyn had some sadness for Lily in her voice. "I see. Did whatever was going to happen happen yet?"

"That it did, but we haven't run across each other just yet. I hope that day comes soon. It's been far too long." Lily sighed as she looked downwards at the oak table's surface.

Evelyn asked her what the first thing she would do when she saw him.

The emerald in Lily's eyes brightened suddenly. "I'd run up to him and jump, locking myself in place with my legs around his waist while he embraced me in his arms."

"Suddenly, you not going after Seth makes a little more sense," Evelyn said.

"Just because I lost track of him, that doesn't mean I'm going to stop living. It does take me a while to find someone. I like to get to know a person I'm interested in first and who they are. Their likes and dislikes. Their wants. Their needs. Their desires. Their fears. What brings them joy. What makes them tick. The process takes quite some time, but, when I do find someone suitable, I thoroughly enjoy myself."

"It's not such a bad thing that it takes you long to find someone, Lily. At least you know what you're looking for."

Lily looked directly into Evelyn's bright blue eyes. The emerald within sparkled. "Truer words. Truer words."

Evelyn looked over and noticed Seth and another waitress making their way over to their table. The two placed the food on the table in front of the respective recipients. The waitress picked up the empty appetizer plates and walked away while Seth asked if they needed anything else. Evelyn decided to add some ground black pepper onto her pasta primavera. Jesse motioned with his hands that he was fine while Lily verbally told Seth the same. Seth left the table with a flushed smile toward Lily, who was smiling coyly back. With that done, the triumvirate was left to their banquet and their growing conversation.

Three

Evelyn came bursting into the cafeteria. She looked around until she found Lily, who was seated at a bistro table all by herself reading a magazine. "You'll never guess what!"

Lily put the gardening magazine down on the table. She was about to ask what, but Evelyn's excitement interrupted her before she had the chance.

"Take a look at this." She placed out her left hand.

Lily noticed a ring on the fourth digit. "You're kidding me? He finally caved?"

"It was actually his idea."

Lily stood up and hugged Evelyn. "When did all of this happen?"

"Not more than twenty minutes ago." Evelyn was blushing. "I just got off my shift, and I was ready to come down here when this boy, who was no older than five or six, suddenly showed up behind me while I was waiting for the lift. He tugged at me so I would turn around and told me that he had something to say to me. Before I could ask him what, he giggled, gave me a soft kick to the shin, turned, and sprinted for the stairwell. Naturally, I followed him to the next floor. He ran down the hallway and into a room, cornering himself. I was about to give him a lecture on how it wasn't nice to kick people in the shins when he pointed behind me. I turned around. There was Jesse, on one knee, with a single rose and a jewellery box. I couldn't believe it. I still can't."

"I'm so happy for the two of you." Lily embraced Evelyn once more.

They leaned back from each other.

"I think I'm still in shock. Like it hasn't really hit me just yet, so, before I totally lose my composure, my first duty is to pick a maid of honour. Lily, would you be mine?"

Lily looked Evelyn straight in her bright blue eyes. "I'd be more than happy to be with you on your special day and play second fiddle, but we've only known each other for a couple months now. Are you sure?"

Evelyn nodded. "More than anything."

Lily smiled. "So when's the big date?" she asked as they both sat down at the bistro table. "Has it been set yet?"

"Sometime next year during the summer."

"I take it you're going to be hiring a judge to perform the ceremony, considering your beliefs?"

Evelyn shook her head. "Actually no."

Lily seemed confused.

"He has a friend who's a cruise ship captain. He confirmed it with him to make sure he was actually certified and where he could perform. When the liner gets the schedule for next year, we'll get a list of prospective dates. We're thinking somewhere around the Caribbean."

Lily's eyes widened. She became very anxious and began to sweat. "So the wedding's going to be at sea?"

"Is that a problem?"

"The ocean and I tend to not get along."

Evelyn noticed the sweat on Lily's forehead. "I must admit, my stomach sometimes takes a turn or two on a boat," she said in an attempt to calm down Lily.

"It's not the motion sickness. It's more of an immense fear." Lily's hands started to shake.

Evelyn was growing very concerned for her. "Are you okay?"

"I'm fine, Evelyn. I'm sorry, but I think I have to decline your offer."

Evelyn had this heartbroken look. Lily's eyes wandered around the cafeteria to find something she could focus on. "It's not like I haven't traveled on boats before, but I only travel on deck when I absolutely have to. When I do, I'm usually drunk or self-medicated in order to get through the trip. I don't want to be like that during your big day. It wouldn't be proper."

Evelyn still had that look of despair, but she understood. She noticed Lily's arms had now begun to shake. Talking to her slowly to try to help calm her down, she asked her why she was so afraid of the water.

"I never used to be. I used to love the water. I even had a house near there at one time, but there was this one particular, sudden storm. I was on this raft and—"

Evelyn took her hands and placed Lily's shaking ones in between hers. She looked down at the table and noticed the magazine. "I never knew you were a gardener."

Lily looked at Evelyn and thanked her for switching the topic with her eyes. Her shaking started to recede. "It's more of a pastime than anything else."

Lily revealed she enjoyed growing flowers over fruits and vegetables. She told Evelyn the types of flowers she liked to grow in her garden. She named many different varieties but informed Evelyn that she took pleasure in growing carnations, specifically those of deep red, pink, and purple.

The emerald in Lily's eyes lit up suddenly. "I almost forgot to tell you." She was no longer shaking. "I finished emptying those boxes. Now that I'm finally settled and seeing how we have big news to celebrate, you two should come over this weekend. It's perfect timing, and I'd love to have you. Is he still dying to see the place?"

"You have no idea! He's pestered me on more than a few occasions about your settling and moving status. This would make his day, probably more so than the engagement."

Evelyn laughed playfully. Lily smiled with closed lips.

"I'll ask Jesse, but I already know his answer. Is Saturday good for you?"

Lily nodded. "I can work my schedule around it." She smiled. "It'll be great to have some company over for a—" Lily's pager went off, interrupting the conversation. "I guess I have to run. Just get back to me on the details for Saturday."

"Will do."

Lily grabbed her gardening magazine, congratulated Evelyn once more, and began heading toward the stairs. Evelyn decided to stay seated at the bistro table while she waited for Jesse. After about ten minutes, she saw him enter the cafeteria.

"There you are!"

Evelyn ran and jumped onto Jesse, locking herself in place with her legs around his waist. "I've been waiting for you." She eagerly kissed his lips before she put herself down.

"Well, you wouldn't have had to if you didn't take off like that." Jesse looked around the cafeteria. "So where's Lily anyhow? I'm assuming that's why you rushed down here so quickly?"

With hand in hand, they turned and started to make their way out the hospital and toward the parking lot.

"Her pager went off so she had to go."

"Did you ask her?"

Evelyn nodded.

"And?"

"She was very excited and accepted my offer. Then she found out the wedding would be at sea and changed her mind."

"Not a nautical person, huh?"

Evelyn looked down. "Guess not."

"Motion sickness or something?"

"I thought so at first myself, but, the longer we were talking about it, she began to sweat and shake. I thought she was going to throw up or pass out or something."

"I see," Jesse said with some subtle disappointment in his voice. "Is there any way she could make it though?"

She shook her head. "It's not likely. She could, but she'll have to be self-medicated for the entire thing and says it would not be proper for such an event. Her conviction will not allow her to take one step onto that boat."

Jesse sighed, albeit silently and under his own breath. "Who's your next choice?"

Evelyn jested that her next pick would be his sister, if he had one, as opposed to two younger brothers.

"Okay," he said. "I'll call up my parents and give them a stern talking to."

"Jerk." She gave him a lighthearted jab to his shoulder with her free hand. "I was thinking about asking Tamara. We have a fairly good relationship and I see her as a mother figure but, I'm still not sure." Jesse could tell she had really wanted Lily to be there. He really wanted her to be there as well but he wouldn't tell that to Evelyn. He went in front of her and poked her on the nose. She smiled hesitantly.

"Don't worry, buckaroo. We'll think of something. There's plenty of time left. Still, it's strange that Lily is afraid of the water, seeing how it's a big religious symbol. I mean, if even I know that, I'm sure she must."

"She said she never used to be though. It was all thanks to this one particular storm. I'm not sure of the details, as she was really starting to freak out, so I switched the topic. In doing so, I found out some news."

Jesse became intrigued. "And what news would this be?"

"She's finished moving everything around at her place. Because of this and our engagement, we're going over on Saturday."

Jesse could not contain his excitement. "Hot damn! Really? She's finally settled? It's about bloody time."

"Why are you so interested in her place? For that matter, why are you so interested in houses in general? It's been more so lately over the past year, and I've always been curious about it."

Jesse put both of his hands away from him, palms exposed. "What? A guy can't be interested in interior design?"

Evelyn took a small step forward and looked him in his chestnut-coloured eyes.

"Not going to work, is it?"

Evelyn placed her left index finger on the middle of his chest. "No, sir."

Jesse shook his head with his eyes closed as a smile began to form and brighten his face.

"It's because our apartment, although lovely, is so small. We could probably fit our entire place into one room of hers."

Jesse turned Evelyn around so he was now behind her. He wrapped his arms around her. "And besides," he lowered his hands and let them rest on her stomach, "we're going to need a bigger place eventually."

She blushed. "Someday, yes, but that day won't be for a while. You used to be so against it though. What's changed?"

"We were young. We still are, but, in these past couple months, I've been giving it a lot more thought. Besides, we do have to keep the species and our bloodlines going. It's our duty to our race."

Evelyn rolled her bright blue eyes. "I should have figured that would be your response."

"Tell me you don't want kids."

"You know that I do. It's just—"

Jesse cut her off. "And now so do I. In about five to ten years, but still—"

Evelyn stopped walking, turned to face him, and kissed his lips. "Who are you, and what have you done with my boyfriend … I mean fiancé, you creepshow?" She stuck out her tongue at him.

Jesse smirked. "He's right here, although now he has come to his senses. I don't know why, but it's been building for some time. Maybe the job has finally gotten to me. You have experience with them when they are little ones and I do when they're a little older. I think we'd be great parents."

Evelyn faced forward once more and placed her head under Jesse's chin. He kissed her neck, and they continued toward the car. He opened the door for her and then climbed in the driver's seat. He put the keys into the ignition but did not start the car.

"So where are we going?" he asked. "Straight home to celebrate? Go for dinner? We've never tried champagne before. This is the perfect time and we can see if we can pop a balloon with the cork."

Evelyn smiled. "Dinner sounds great, you goof, but I'd like to share the big news with my parents first, if you don't mind."

Jesse placed his right hand over her left and soothingly rubbed his thumb back and forth.

"Like you even have to ask. Do you want to go pick up some flowers before we head to the cemetery?"

"Nah. There's still plenty left there."

"Okay."

Jesse removed his hand from on top of hers and turned on the engine.

Four

Lily answered the door. Her long, soot black hair was straight, down, and free-flowing. Her dangle earrings were long, straight, singular, and silver. She was wearing a one-piece, silk, black halter dress with a below-knee handkerchief hem. It was full in front, open-backed, and tied around her neckline. Her pure silver, Knights Templars cross fashioned from a Cross Fitchy was still visible as it used the silk collar as its background. All of this was accompanied by stiletto shoes, whose thin straps wrapped around her ankles.

"Welcome to my kingdom," she said as Jesse and Evelyn stepped onto the marble mosaic floor in the main foyer.

They immediately noticed an eight-point compass rose resting before the central grand oak staircase. The newel-to-newel railings were curved as one would make his way up to an intermediate landing where the stairs split both right and left. The two flights opened up to a landing that connected the second floor to the house. The second floor had a balcony overlooking the doorway and was supported by columns resting underneath it. The balcony passed over the stairwell, helping to connect the left and right sides of the floor. Other than this, one could reach the right or left sides of the second floor via two land bridges. One of these was straight and ran horizontally down the middle. With the railings that continued from the staircase and the gaps on the left and right, one may consider it a middle balcony. The other bridge was more of a curve that began at the far end of the floor. Each side had one passage and linked with the first horizontal land bridge. These corridors helped to lead one to the other sanctuaries of the house.

"Well I'll be damned," Jesse said with much delight. "This was definitely worth the wait."

Lily smiled in the upper right corner of her mouth. "You can explore the house if you wish, Jesse. Just try not to get lost."

Jesse was already making his way toward the stairwell. Lily motioned Evelyn to follow her. On their way to the kitchen, they took a right off the foyer and walked onto hardwood floors and through a parlour. Evelyn noticed a lot of classic furniture inside this parlour. A single-ended sofa placed in front of an intricately carved marble walk-in fireplace caught her bright blue eyes most. She could not make out the intricate designs of the fireplace from where she was walking, but she did notice a knight's arming sword mounted above the mantle.

Once the two girls reached the kitchen, Evelyn had a seat on a barstool that seemed somewhat out of place. It was next to one of two hexagon-shaped butcher block stations. The station itself was directly connected to the floor and littered with books and what appeared to be a deck of Tarot cards.

Lily stood on the other side of the butcher block station. "I managed to get my hands on some of the drink of kings."

Evelyn looked at her, puzzled.

"I just need to remember where I put those flutes."

"Oh!" Evelyn said as she clued in. "Champagne."

Lily laughed. "Yes, champagne. From Reims." Lily began checking the cupboards below the butcher block station, which was cluttered with books, for the flutes before moving onto the cupboards above the long-running counter spaces. "Sorry about the mess, Evelyn. I lost track of time. I really wanted to put those books back in the library and the stool back at the bar before you two showed up."

Evelyn modestly placed her arms forward in front of her chest. "Don't worry about it. Besides, I'm used to clutter, and you seemed to still have had enough time to dress up even though there was no need. I mean, look at us. We're both in jeans."

"Who's dressing up?"

The phone, which was hanging next to the refrigerator, started to ring.

"Will you excuse me for a second?"

"Sure."

Lily stopped her search for the flutes and went to answer the phone. As she was walking away, Evelyn noticed a tattoo on the inside part of her right ankle. It appeared as if it were fashioned in the shape of a serpent wrapped around a harvesting scythe, but she could not be sure as the ankle straps overlapped it in its center. Evelyn looked down at the clutter before her and started to sift through it. She noticed a card with a man in a chariot, which was being drawn by two sphinxes. The card displayed the roman numeral of seven above it. It was sitting there as if almost deliberately placed. She slid the card to the right a little bit with her thumb to see what book it was resting on. It was the Bible. Her bright blue eyes shifted around the table and glanced at the other books scattered throughout the deck of cards. She noticed *Paradise Lost, Pilgrim's Progress, The Confessions of Saint Augustine, The Inferno, Faust, Frankenstein, Lyrical Ballads 1798,* and *Beowulf,* but something seemed odd to her. They all seemed as if they were first editions, as she did not quite recognize the English language to those that were actually written in English. She could tell they had been used prior, but, despite this, the books were well taken care of.

She began looking around the rest of the room. The other butcher block station was right across from the stove. A bucket filled with ice and water was resting in the center of it. As she was looking at the counter space, she noticed there were no appliances. Instead, the counter space held spice racks, herbs, and containers with what she assumed were flour and sugar. The sink was empty, and a window reigned just above it. There was an empty glass, which seemed a little stained from the empty bottle of red wine that was resting next to the sink. Evelyn heard Lily say that she would see someone later before hanging up the phone. She had this beaming smile on her face as she opened the refrigerator. She took the champagne and placed it in the bucket on the second station. She checked under this butcher block station, and Evelyn lost sight of her.

"Aha!" Lily exclaimed. "Here they are!" She became visible once again and put three crystal flutes on the station next to the bucket. "Now all we have to do is to wait for that fiancé of yours to find us, and we're all set." Lily started walking back toward Evelyn.

"Let him take his time. Who was that on the phone? I'm thinking it was someone important, considering that smile of yours."

Lily kept her smile, but did not blush. "That was Seth."

"As in the cute waiter from the Ivy?"

"The very same. He was just calling before the lunch rush."

Evelyn had some excitement in her voice. "When did all of this happen?"

"A few weeks ago. I went back to the Ivy for brunch, and we just hit it off, even more so than we had previously when we went."

"Is he coming tonight after his shift?"

"No, he doesn't know about this. It's your night. I don't wish for anything to overshadow it."

"You could never do such a thing." She stood up and hugged Lily. "Besides, now we can double."

"Let's see what happens first."

Evelyn looked a little confused as she took her seat. "You don't want to double with us? There's safety in numbers."

"That is true, but I'm more of a private girl when it comes to situations like this. I prefer to walk down a beach or through a park in the middle of a quiet night with my beau as opposed to a double. Maybe find a swing set in the park and just sit there quietly or gain momentum as we swing the pendulum back and forth while reaching for the heavens." Lily continued to trail off. "A quiet night alone where we don't have to act like we're on display, laying in each other's arms with a glass of wine and a roaring fire. Me, wearing nothing except for a fur coat and some silk or maybe satin underwear."

Evelyn's bright blue eyes started to look downwards. "Wish mine would do things like that with me." Her bright blue eyes returned to Lily. "I never realized you were such the romantic."

"What can I say?" She laughed jovially. "Old habits die hard." The emerald sparkled. "Why don't you try to coerce him into trying some of those things? A swing in a park is inexpensive, and you know I have many more ideas that I can give to you."

Evelyn laughed, but it sounded more like a gibe. "He's just not that kind of guy. More down-to-earth, not seeing the beauty in everything type."

"Well, from that dinner conversation and conversations since, he appears to be a very literal person, but I'm not around when the doors are closed so I didn't want to claim to know."

"I never thought of it that way before." Her bright blue eyes started to wander. "He is very literal. Maybe it's just the differences between men and women. I mean, he's open, caring, and loving, and now he wants to start a family whereas he never wanted to before. It's just … I don't really know anymore." Evelyn lowered her bright blue eyes. "At least you may get those things with Seth, considering the relationship is new and everything." Her eyes levelled back up.

"Maybe. But who knows if he'll do any of it anyhow."

"Yeah," Evelyn sarcastically replied, "because I'm sure there's no way Seth wouldn't want to see you in just a fur coat and panties."

The two girls shared a laugh. They heard a voice entering from the side.

"I hope that laughing isn't at my expense." Jesse went to kiss Evelyn on the top of her head.

"No, no, honey," Evelyn reassured him. "Don't you worry."

Lily moved her eyes slightly to Evelyn's left. "Welcome back. Glad to see you didn't get lost."

Jesse looked toward Lily. "It would be a little hard. The whole place seems to be interconnected, like some sort of naturally occurring cave system. You have quite the house here."

"Why thank you," she answered humbly.

Evelyn turned in her seat and looked up at Jesse. "Hey, hun, you'll never guess what."

Jesse looked down at Evelyn, waiting for her response.

"Do you remember Seth?"

"The waiter?"

"Yeah. Guess who he's dating?"

Jesse looked at Lily and noticed her smile. "What a lucky bastard."

Evelyn gave him a playful push. "And just what is that supposed to mean?"

"Well, you know. Not nearly as lucky as I am. I can tell you that much. I mean, it's just, you know what I mean, right?"

Evelyn rolled her bright blue eyes. "Ya, ya. I know. The house. The car. The style. The fashion. Don't freak out, hun."

Jesse breathed a sigh of relief.

"Okay, you two. It's time to open that bottle."

She started to make her way over to the second butcher block. Evelyn stood up from her barstool and walked with Jesse, hand in hand, toward Lily.

Jesse looked at Evelyn. "What bottle?"

"Lily bought a bottle of champagne for the occasion."

"You know, we've always wanted to try that, Lily. How did you know?"

"It's my job to know such things." Lily gently opened the bottle. She laughed. "That and it is a toasting occasion." Lily filled the three flutes two-thirds of the way. Lily put her flute in the air first, and the other two followed suit. "Here is to happy endings and new beginnings."

The three clinked their flutes together after Lily's toast and drank their champagne.

"I think I could acquire a taste for this stuff," Jesse said.

Lily asked, "Do you want to be topped off.

"Like you even have to ask?"

Lily filled Jesse's glass two-thirds of the way up once more.

Evelyn was looking at the bubbles in her flute. "Is it true that champagne gets you drunk faster?"

"Well, there's one way you can test it out."

She rolled her bright blue eyes. "I'm sure you'd love that, wouldn't you?"

Lily observed the couple.

"Well, you don't have that much of a tolerance to begin with," Jesse answered.

"Sounds like a challenge to me."

"I'd take you on that challenge, but how are we going to get home?"

"You two needn't worry about that," Lily said. "I have a few spare rooms. It's not like this is a small house."

"So it's settled then," Evelyn confirmed.

Jesse advocated that they move over to the bar.

"There's a bar here?"

"Sure is, Evey. In the living room."

"But I didn't see one when we past through it to get to the kitchen."

"I have a second parlour," Lily told her. "The bar is in there."

"Well then, what are we waiting for?" Evelyn asked.

Lily grabbed the champagne after placing it back into the ice and water-filled bucket, and the three left the kitchen. Evelyn and Jesse followed Lily back into the foyer. They made their way past the sliding doors that led outside the house and walked into the dining room. A crystal chandelier hung above a long, rectangular oak table that was placed in the center of the room. Around the table were fourteen Queen Anne armchairs with burgundy-coloured velvet backings and cushions. They continued to make their way through the dining room and arrived in the second parlour. Lily took a right when they entered the room and went behind the bar's counter. She placed the champagne bucket down as Jesse and Evelyn took a seat next to each other on the barstools.

"So what can I get you two to start with?"

"A Tom Collins for me," Jesse said.

"And a Brandy Alexander for me," Evelyn added.

Lily mixed the two drinks and refilled the couple's flutes.

"I think that, before we start this," Evelyn said, "I'm going to use the washroom."

Lily pointed toward the staircase. "Second floor on the east wing. Second door on your left.

"Thanks." Evelyn stood up and started to make her way to the staircase.

Lily looked toward Jesse. "Are you really ready to take this on?"

"Sure am," Jesse confidently responded. "She's just trying to show to her big sister that she has chops."

Lily looked directly into Jesse's chestnut-coloured eyes. "Not the drinking contest. The marriage."

"Oh, that."

"When I told you this was more or less it for her, you didn't have to go right out and buy the ring."

He cupped his hands around his crystal glass. "Granted." His eyes lowered into his drink. "But she's more or less it for me, too."

Lily held back her disgust of Jesse's comment. "So you're just going about it because that's it? Doesn't sound heart-filled and romantic to me. You even decided to go with the standard diamond ring. If you wanted to profess your deepest emotions and love toward her, why not go with a ruby or have six stones in the ring?"

"A six-stone engagement ring?"

Lily nodded. "Yes."

"How's that work?"

Lily took Jesse's right hand in her left. She pointed her right index finger over his class ring.

"You place your birthstones here in the center and the birthstones of your parents next to your stone, one to the left and one to the right. Same goes for her side. It's more or less given to show two families merging into one." She removed her hands.

"I like that," admitted Jesse. "But I don't think she needs any reminders of her parents."

She gave him an inquisitive look. "I thought you said she had a close-knit family?"

He had a drink of his Tom Collins. "Yes, had. She doesn't really like to talk about it, but both her parents developed a terminal illness of sorts at different times."

Jesse first told Lily that her mother died of leukemia while Evelyn was in high school. "After that, her father never really recovered, which was a shame considering how nice a guy he was." He placed his glass back on the bar's counter. "I was there with her in the hospital room when he died from cancer. Evey told me he had it on and off his entire life, but, after her mother died, he just seemed to give up the fight." He shook his head sympathetically. "With all that she saw and went through, it's no wonder she pushed their religion and beliefs out of her head. She just couldn't see it anymore."

The emerald illuminated. "So that's what you meant when you said there were no sudden deaths or tragedies while we were at the Ivy."

"I don't even remember saying that. How did you?"

Lily leaned over the bar and closer toward Jesse. "You would be surprised at what I remember. You never did answer my question about the marriage though. Don't go getting married just because you think she deserves it."

Jesse looked at Lily, but not directly at her. "I thought you believed in marriage though."

She looked him in the eyes. "I do, but this isn't marriage. This is compensation and duty all rolled into one."

His eyes slouched downwards toward the bar. "Still, I want to start a family. I'm not in my early twenties anymore, and I'm beginning to settle down. I can't imagine a family without her in it."

"You can still start a family anyhow. Do you really need that ring as a security blanket? When you started dating her five years ago, were you counting on marriage? Did you see it, or want it with her?"

"Not right away, but, after about the year mark, I knew she was the one for me."

"Then why not ask her back then? And you're not allowed to use the lack of money or career as an excuse, seeing how she is the one for you."

Jesse looked down at his drink and pondered Lily's strain of questions. He had no response. He brought his eyes back up and noticed Lily was still looking into his. The emerald within was faintly glistening. Jesse heard footsteps coming down the stairs, but he did not turn around. He continued to stare into Lily's eyes. He quickly drank his Tom Collins and placed the crystal glass back on the bar just before chasing it with his flute of champagne. Evelyn entered the room.

"That's some big vanity mirror you have in there, Lily." She took her seat next to Jesse. "And a claw-foot tub, too. Very nice."

Lily laughed playfully. "Thank you, Evelyn. I'm an old soul with a draw toward the classics."

Evelyn noticed Jesse's empty glasses. "Starting without me?"

Jesse turned his head to his left and looked headlong at Evelyn. "How many times have you started without me?"

Evelyn tried not to blush. "I don't really think that's an issue."

"Sure, sure." He looked down at the empty glass. "I just changed my mind and want something stronger is all." He took a second to think. "Lily?"

"Yes?"

"Any tequila and a shot glass?"

"Sure thing."

Evelyn turned her head to the tender. "Can you make that two shot glasses and some Scotch?"

"Coming right up."

Lily disappeared from sight behind the bar as she opened a drawer for the shot glasses. She reemerged and placed the two shot glasses on the bar. She turned and grabbed the tequila and Scotch from the shelf behind her. She began to pour the drinks. "Now, Evelyn, I have to warn you. This Scotch has been aged around sixty years. Funny thing is that it's the youngest Scotch I have. Just be ready. It may be young, but it still has kick." She finished pouring.

"You're not going to join us?" Evelyn asked.

"Do you really want me involved?"

"Why wouldn't we?" Jesse said.

She smirked. "All right then. But just a warning. No man or woman has ever been able to drink me under the table." Lily turned around and grabbed a bottle of dry gin. She grabbed herself a shot glass and poured.

"An undefeated champ, huh?"

Lily laughed at Jesse's comment. "You have no idea."

Jesse took his shot and Evelyn hers. She chased it with her Alexander while Lily took back her gin.

"More I'm assuming?" Lily asked the couple.

Both Evelyn and Jesse nodded their heads in agreement. Lily poured three more drinks.

"Before I let you two have these, it is still relatively early, but what do you want me to cook for dinner?"

Jesse rolled his eyes. "Well, it can't be anything with meat in it since this one next to me here is a vegetarian."

"I do have pasta."

Evelyn turned her head to Jesse. "Like your taste for flesh is any better."

"Tomato, basil, and mushroom sauce for starters."

"You'll be passed right out before dinner comes anyway." Jesse took his shot.

"Can even bake a few potatoes."

"And you won't be?" Evelyn took hers.

Lily refilled their shot glasses. "With a nice salad and vegetables."

"Where's the romance, Jesse?" Another shot of Scotch gone.

"Maybe even some wild rice as a pleasant side dish."

"What's happened to the view of raising a family? What was with that 'It's just' comment you began to make a few days ago?" Another shot of tequila swallowed.

Lily refilled the glasses once more. "And a roll of garlic bread."

"Literal prick." Evelyn took the shot glass back and reached for her flute.

"Some vanilla ice crème with some crème de menthe poured over it as dessert."

"Repressive, inquisitive wench." Jesse emptied his shot glass.

"All right, children." Lily snapped her fingers and drew their attention toward her. "Why all this bickering? This is your day. Be happy. Granted, marriage is full of bickering, but it's also supposed to be fun. One spouse trying to outdo the other in an unending lovers' game. You've been engaged for less than a week, and this is how you're going about it? How are you going to survive?" Lily poured three more shots.

"Maybe we won't," Evelyn grimly stated.

The emerald gleamed as she looked into Evelyn's bright blue eyes. "Don't be so negative, Evelyn. You two are a good couple. Better than most I've seen, and I've seen a lot in my time. You need to at least give it a shot. I just think the marriage has finally hit home. Don't worry. It'll pass, and everything will be fine. If anything, this little bump in the road will reinforce your relationship."

Both Jesse and Evelyn perked up from Lily's words of encouragement and kissed a lover's kiss. They grabbed their flutes and crisscrossed their drinking arms together. Lily smirked on the right side of her face and emptied the gin from her glass. The couple leaned back. Lily looked at their empty glasses and asked if they wanted a refill, to which they both agreed.

Five

Lily was standing in the nursery. She was looking at a child placed in one of the hospital's bassinets. She started to run her hand down the side of the chubby child's blue blanket. Her fingers began to creep from the blanket to the child's stomach, who then laughed as he found the motion ticklish. Just as she was about to sigh, she became startled from a knock on the glass. She turned around and noticed Evelyn waving from the other side. Lily noticed she was not in a smock, so she knew Evelyn was just getting into her shift. She waved back and made her way out of the nursery to meet her. They hugged each other.

"I heard you spend your breaks in the nursery now, but it's just one of those things you need to see for yourself."

"It's soothing really, but I'm not on break. I finished my shift about twenty minutes ago. I just haven't made my way to the lockers yet. Anyway, how are things, Evelyn? It's been a while."

"I know! Our schedules just don't seem to sync lately, and these wedding plans are taking up the rest of my free time. Who thought it would take so much effort to get like fifty people on a boat?"

Lily smirked at Evelyn's comment. "At least your jitters are over with."

Evelyn's face lit up. "I can't thank you enough for that. Who knows what would have happened if it continued to fester. It was a bit embarrassing, having it come out in front of you like that, but, to be honest, I'm kind of glad we were there with you so you could calm us down. I'm sure Jesse and I would have missed the reason as to why if you didn't get involved those couple weeks ago."

"No thanks are needed." Lily shook her head modestly. "It's what I do. Just remember that, as the date gets closer, it may hit home again. But enough of the jitters. Since the big day is getting closer, is your father ready to give you away to Jesse yet?"

Evelyn twitched slightly.

Lily saw this and ran her hand softly down Evelyn's arm. "What's wrong, hun?" The emerald quickly made its way from side to side as she looked into Evelyn's bright blue eyes, which were slowly starting to sink.

"Well, the thing is that it isn't possible." A tear trickled down her cheek.

Lily's face became suddenly distraught. She did not say anything. Through her tears, Evelyn told Lily the story about her parents.

Lily embraced her. "I had no idea. I didn't mean to bring it up." She wiped away Evelyn's tears.

"That's okay." Evelyn sniffled. "You didn't know."

"Still, are you okay?"

"I'm fine." Evelyn sniffled once again. "I really am. The actual wedding day may be a little hard, but I'll get through it."

The emerald sparked. "Well, if you do happen to cry, everyone will assume it as tears of joy."

Evelyn seemed to perk up a little. "I never thought of it that way."

"Just make sure to keep your eyes bright and catch them in that Caribbean sunshine," advised Lily. "If you do start to cry, those wedding guests will be saddened yet wiser for knowing what love actually is."

"You think?"

"I'd put money on it."

Evelyn's sunny disposition returned. They began to walk toward the locker room.

"Do you have a maid of honour yet?"

"I'm going to ask Tamara about it. Although, seeing how she is married and everything, she would be my matron of honour. I know some girls have both matron and maid, but one is good enough for me."

"How about a wedding dress? Have you picked one out?"

"I haven't even gotten around to that yet."

Lily stopped Evelyn and faced her right outside the doors to the locker room. The emerald flashed. "We're going to take tomorrow off and go do some dress shopping for you."

"That sounds fantastic Lily, but what about Ms. Fraystl and my shift?"

She placed her hands on Evelyn's shoulders. "Just leave Ms. Fraystl to me." Lily took her hands off Evelyn's shoulders. She leaned back a little bit and opened the door for her. "I'd say we go tonight after you have done your shift, but Seth is coming to pick me up soon. Definitely tomorrow though."

Evelyn reached her locker and started to strip down. Lily did the same, taking off her smock at her locker. As Evelyn was taking off her blouse, she asked Lily, "How's Seth?"

"He's a sweetheart." Lily began to dress herself by pulling up a dark-laced, trimmed nylon stocking to her right thigh.

"Is that so?"

"He gets this certain flush in his cheeks when he's around me. It's cute," she said with some hesitation. Next was the left thigh.

"I sense a 'but' coming."

"But I wish he would get out of this schoolboy crush phase. I think it's because the relationship is still new."

Evelyn was sliding out of her jeans. "If he doesn't get out of that phase, what do you plan on doing?"

"I guess I'll have to leave him." Lily slipped into a blue-and-white, strapless sundress. "I don't really want to, but I can't stay in daycare land forever. Cute is fine for a while, but I want romance and a man."

Evelyn turned from her locker. "How do you think he would take it? If you were to suddenly end things?"

"No idea. With my history of strange effects on men, who knows what will happen."

Evelyn turned back into her locker to reach for her work clothes. "Have you two at least slept together yet?"

"Sure have."

Lily put her hair down and ran her hands through it. Her Knights Templars cross swayed back and forth around her neck as her hands moved her head. It made a resonating noise as it came into contact with the silver chain it was connected to.

"And …" Evelyn inquired, as she was dying to know.

Lily bent over toward the lower part of her locker. "Not that I'm one to kiss and tell, but I've had better. To be fair though, I've had a lot worse. He's an advanced intermediate."

She took her black ankle-strapped stiletto shoes from the locker's floor and closed it.

"That sounds good, right?"

Lily nodded her head. "Definitely. The thing with intermediates is that they're still malleable to that desired ending state. No one will ever be as good as my husband though. He reached his potential early on, even before I met him. Maybe I'm just biased because he has done great things.

He was clever and good at holding me in anticipation. I have no idea why but …" She bit the bottom of her lip. "Anticipation can really get me going. I think that's the reason." Lily's head drooped a little as she let out a small sigh. "I'll never have that love or passion toward anyone else, but c'est la vie. With Seth, the fact we have been together, coupled with my effect on men, may be enough to drive him over the edge. It wouldn't be the first time."

Evelyn was starting to put on the smock and the rest of her work clothes. Lily sat down on the bench and put on her shoes. "This may be a little personal, but do you mind if I were to ask you something?"

Lily looked up from putting on her shoes. "Sure."

"Would you leave Seth or any other man you were with if you ran into your husband?"

The emerald flickered vibrantly. "In a heartbeat," she said instantly. "I know that may sound callous, but the heart wants what she wants. This torch will never extinguish."

"I see." Evelyn's bright blue eyes shifted across the ground as she tied back her hair. "I hope Jesse and I have even a little of that love in five to ten years." Evelyn closed her locker door. She took a seat next to Lily.

Lily placed her right hand on Evelyn's left shoulder and started to rub it. "Weather the storm, and it will last for the rest of your life. I'm living, breathing proof of that. Just don't be so anxious, and you'll be fine. How's Jesse doing with this whole thing anyhow?"

"Jesse? Jesse's content for the most part. His family is overjoyed at the fact we will finally all be family soon."

"Sounds like you think he's just marrying you for marriage sake."

Evelyn's bright blue eyes wandered up and down and from side to side in the locker room in a sporadic fashion. "Well, I just don't know anymore." She breathed in heavily. "Do I really need the safety of that ring?" Evelyn still insisted that she wanted to be his wife, as she loved him and his family and couldn't dream of being with anyone else, but her doubts were continuing to grow. "Worlds are colliding inside my head."

Lily placed Evelyn's right hand in between both of hers. "Have you talked to him about this?"

"How can I? My mind changes every moment." The emerald watched her bright blue eyes as she continued. "One minute, I can't think about being anything else than Mrs. Jesse Chamberlain with a couple kids and a white picket fence. The next minute, I can't believe that this is it for me. It's just very surreal."

The emerald moved from side to side. "Did you only accept his invitation because you thought you deserved or were entitled to it?"

Evelyn hesitated at first. "I guess on some level, but he does have my heart, and my heart wants the marriage."

"The heart can be deceiving though. It takes a lot of retrospect to distinguish it from a flickering candle to a full-out blaze."

Evelyn took a moment. "Are you saying I should break off or, at the very least, postpone the wedding?"

The emerald moved back and forth. "I'm not saying that. Only you will truly know what you have to do. At the end of the day, no matter who you talk to, the decision comes down to you, but, if you want my advice …"

"I do."

"Let the heart win out over the head. The head can be quite the pain. Since you actually have one on your shoulders, it may lead you down the wrong path. Thought can be a prison, but you should cage yourself inside of it in order to see and understand. Sure, you may end up regretting certain choices, but at least you will have lived and no regret, even if it takes years to form, will be able to take away from that."

Evelyn's face brightened a little. "You sure do make quite a bit of sense there."

"Remember …" She removed her hands from Evelyn's. "I do believe in love and what it can do to a person, no matter how shallow or deep it may be."

Evelyn looked to the ground. "You don't see much of it these days."

"I know." Lily laughed. "I'm such a dinosaur."

Evelyn seemed to smile. Lily looked at the clock in the locker room, which was hanging above the plastered sink. "I didn't realize how long I was in the nursery. Was more than twenty minutes, that's for sure." Lily stood up. "I have to run."

"I'll see you to the lift."

Evelyn stood up. The two made their way out of the locker room and toward the elevators. "When were you supposed to meet Seth?"

"In about five minutes from now. Down in the cafeteria."

"Big date tonight?"

"No idea. Just playing it by ear."

They turned a corner.

"So tell me about Tamara," Lily said. "Why her?"

Evelyn turned her head to her. "I sort of see her as a mother figure. She helped show me the ropes around here when I first started."

"That makes sense."

Evelyn turned her head back to the hallway. "Plus, she's been married for some forty-odd years. I feel as if it would be a blessing to have someone who has been married for that long as my maid ... er ... matron of honour."

"What does her husband do?"

"He's a rabbi."

"A rabbi, you say." Lily quirked an eyebrow. "That's interesting."

"I think the two of you would get along great, considering your background and thoughts on religion and spirituality."

Lily smirked. "It is possible but highly unlikely."

"Why?"

"Although I love talking to religious officials, most of them do not see things in the same light that I do. The church, or rather, any religious sanctuary of public worship, and I do not get along." She shrugged. "Differing points of view, I guess."

"What do you mean?"

"They're wolves in the guise of shepherds. Religion isn't faith, but, somewhere along the way, the two became one, and people no longer know how to properly separate the two."

Lily and Evelyn emerged at the end of the hallway that led to the nurses' station. They walked about halfway down the corridor, where they could see into the waiting area. Past the nurses' station, Seth was sitting there patiently around a small, rectangular coffee table that housed a clutter of magazines. Lily stopped Evelyn.

"I thought you were meeting him in the cafeteria?"

"I was." Lily huffed with some small annoyance. "See, this is how it starts. He's too eager, and he is not listening. He needs to learn to take his time and be patient."

Seth noticed Lily and stood up. She smiled and walked over to meet him. She passed by Tamara, who was seated behind the reception desk of the nurses' station and Bruce and Ryan, who were standing guard near it.

"Hey, love," Seth said.

Lily put her right hand on her hip. "What happened to the cafeteria?"

"I got off a little bit early and decided I should come surprise you, so ... well ... umm ... I guess ... surprise!"

"Gawky maniac."

Seth looked down a little with his light-coloured eyes. She took her right index finger, placed it under his chin, and raised it slightly. She looked up and into his eyes. The luminous emerald pierced through his momentary sadness.

"But you're my gawky maniac." She kissed his right cheek and leaned in to whisper in his ear before kissing it softly. His face became flustered and shone due to what she whispered. She leaned back from him.

"You remember Evelyn?"

"How could I forget about me Mum?"

Evelyn smiled and waved. Lily pointed forward and showed him most of the other employees she worked with.

"The plump woman behind the desk is Tamara. This short, little, bald man here is Bruce. The man with the crew cut and full jaw is Ryan. We could stay longer for you to get to know them better, but you've gotten a good enough look, plus your mother over there has some important business to attend to."

Seth looked over as if he was going to ask her.

"I'll tell you about it later. Are you ready to go love?"

"Sure am," he enthusiastically replied.

Lily looked over toward Evelyn. "Remember, Evelyn. Tomorrow."

"I'll remember."

Lily took Seth's hand. They turned around and went to the elevator. Lily pressed the button to summon it. Seth looked over at her. "What's tomorrow?"

"Just some girl stuff." Lily looked up at him. "Nothing to concern yourself over."

The elevator made its standard pinging noise, and the doors opened. They walked in, and Lily pushed the button for the main floor. The elevator closed its doors. Evelyn looked over and went to the reception desk.

"Hi, Tamara."

Tamara looked up from some medical papers. "Hi, dear. How are you doing today?"

"Good. Pretty good. Are you busy? There's something really important that I need to ask you."

Six

Evelyn was squeamishly staring at a king cobra as it was slithering around its terrarium. She reluctantly came with Jesse to the special reptilian exhibit at the Natural History Museum.

"So tell me again, Jesse. Why are we here at this indoor exhibition? You know I hate things with scaly skin and things that slither. Couldn't we have gone to a dog show instead? At least they're furry and friendly."

Jesse did not look back to answer as he was looking into a terrarium. "Most of those dogs at those shows are snooty, spoiled brats. Besides, it's a limited time only. Isn't that reason enough? They can't hurt you. They're scattered throughout this museum in big glass terrariums."

She shuddered. "It still doesn't make them any less creepy."

Evelyn looked around the room, trying to find something else to focus on as Jesse was reading a fact sheet next to the tank of the horned lizard. As her bright blue eyes sifted throughout the crowd, her vision focused on a woman standing in front of a tank that ran the entire length of the wall. Evelyn tugged on Jesse's arm. He turned around.

"You see that woman over there?"

Jesse looked around in the general direction Evelyn was pointing to.

"She's in a red turtleneck, a black pleated skirt, and a scarf that's wrapped around her neck."

"Yeah, I see her. What of it?"

"If you uncurled her hair and made it straight and put a silver cross where that scarf is, wouldn't that be Lily?"

Jesse took his time and looked her up and down. "There's a good chance it is. Maybe if we could get a side view of her, I could give you a better answer."

"I figured you of all people would be able to tell her from just her backside."

"Like you're one to talk."

She ignored Jesse's comment. "I thought she said she was busy with Seth today."

Jesse shrugged. "Maybe they're meeting here, or maybe something came up. Why don't we go over and see if it's actually her?"

He started to walk forward, but she grabbed his arm. "No, no. Let's stay here and watch."

"Paranoid much?"

"No. Just wondering why she's not with Seth."

The woman stepped forward and placed her right hand, palm open flush onto the glass of the tank. She closed her eyes and tilted her head downward as if in prayer.

Evelyn let go of Jesse's arm and looked at him. "That's a little weird, right?"

"So she likes snakes," Jesse said in defence of the woman. "There's nothing wrong with that. Didn't you say she had some sort of snake tattoo on her ankle or something when you were checking her out?"

"Yeah."

He looked inquiringly at her. "But?"

"She's done this before."

Jesse scratched the top of his forehead. "How do you mean?"

"The first day I met her, she did the same thing on the glass window that separates the nursery."

He looked back toward the woman. "Well, she does adore children. Didn't you say that she often spends her breaks entertaining them and making sure they're safe?

"Yeah."

"So, if she likes snakes, wouldn't it make sense that she did the same? To be close to them? She bowed her head. It kind of makes it seem that she feels sorry for them being in captivity."

The woman took her hand off the glass. She turned and headed for the exit.

"That is definitely her," said Evelyn.

"We're going to be following her now, right?"

"Why do you ask questions you already know the answer to?"

Evelyn stood up and began to follow the woman. Jesse stayed a few feet behind, but still kept up with her.

"She won't like this if she finds out, Evey. Why do you need to pursue this?"

"I need to see why she's not with Seth."

Jesse seemed to sigh. "Why do you have this urge to know everything? Don't you think that some things are better left to the imagination?"

Evelyn did not answer him.

"Besides, she's an open person, and you two are like sisters. Don't you think she'd tell you if something bad was going on between her and Seth?"

"More than likely, but we're here now."

Evelyn stopped suddenly as the woman made her way down the stairs that led out into the streets. Before she stepped through the doors, she opened the umbrella she was carrying.

"Looks like she left," Jesse stated.

Evelyn stared at him.

"But we don't have an umbrella and have no idea where she's going. We're going to get soaked."

"That's just a chance we'll have to take. Now hurry up. We may lose her."

Evelyn quickly ran down the stairs and out the door. The sky was overcast as the rain was already in heavy downpour. Her hair quickly turned darker in colour because of it. The door opened behind her, and Jesse stepped out.

"Do you see her?"

Evelyn surveyed the streets until she finally spotted her. "Over there."

The woman was crossing the street at a four-point intersection near a newspaper stand.

"If we're going that way," Jesse said, "I'm buying a newspaper for a makeshift umbrella."

Evelyn watched as the woman crossed the street and then crossed the street again. "Let's go." She grabbed Jesse's arm, and they slowly made their way over to the newspaper stand.

"How much?"

The white-bearded clerk wearing thick glasses looked at Jesse. "Four seventy."

"For just one paper?"

"It's no ordinary paper."

"Is that so?"

"Let me let you in on a little secret there, my soaked friend." The clerk leaned on the counter space of his newsstand. "It's also an umbrella."

He held himself in check and reluctantly paid the advantageous clerk. "Fine. Here's five, and you can keep the change, pally."

Jesse turned around and placed the open newspaper above their heads as they waited for the light to change. When it did, the couple crossed with the rest of the walkers. They followed the woman for a good fifteen minutes, staying shy and far enough away to not be seen. Eventually, the woman walked up a set of long, running concrete stairs in her dark brown boots with two-inch heels and headed into a building. The building was made of mostly solid grey-coloured bricks. The structure had many arcs and some inlets high above the entrance in which statues of angels and saints were placed inside. It was St. George's Catholic Church, the largest church in town.

"What day is it?" Evelyn asked.

"It's not Sunday, if that's what you're thinking."

"And it's the middle of the day. There shouldn't be a service now, would there?"

"Like I of all people would know." He turned his head toward Evelyn. "You're not actually thinking of going in there, are you?"

She stared at Jesse.

"We'll be cornering ourselves. What if she sees us? She knows we're not believers. What are we going to say? We just woke up this morning and heard the Good News?"

"Sarcasm isn't going to get us anywhere on this."

Evelyn left the protection of the now-wet and torn newspaper. She made her way up the concrete stairs and looked through the stained glass on the wooden oak doors. She didn't see anyone on the other side so she went in with Jesse right behind her. They turned to their left and walked up a few stairs to an intermediate landing. They stood there and looked ahead while they were dripping onto the carpet runner that made its way from where they were standing to the altar that lay past the open, inner doors and empty rows of pews. Evelyn's bright blue eyes noticed a large, rectangular altarpiece of stained glass that was arced near the top, centered in the wall. It appeared to depict a lineage of persons in an almost treelike form.

Once her bright blue eyes moved their way down the tree and neared the altar, she saw her. She pushed Jesse behind her as she took a couple of steps back down the stairs and hid against the wall before poking her head out slightly from behind it. She looked toward the altar once more and noticed the woman was holding a candle surrounded by a coloured glass container. She placed it amongst the rest of the prominent candles, although it seemed as if it were overshadowing them. She proceeded to the left of the candles and made her way past the altar and into a confessional booth.

"She's going to confession," Evelyn whispered.

Jesse popped his head out from around the corner. "Seriously?"

"Dead."

"Well, maybe she just has things on her mind. Maybe she's using it to clear her conscious, or maybe she's going to use the priest as cheap and free therapy."

"I wonder why."

Jesse sighed. "She's a believer. That's why."

Evelyn shook her head from side to side. "But she doesn't like the church. How'd she put it? It had something to do with wolves looking like shepherds."

"I can see her point on that and how a truly faithful person wouldn't find solace in a place like this."

"Exactly. So then why is she here? More importantly, why is she in a confessional? Something just isn't adding up."

"You'll never find out unless she tells you, but how would you bring it up? Hey, Lily, Jesse and I followed you a few days ago, and I was just curious. What did you say in that confessional?"

Evelyn elbowed Jesse in his stomach without turning and continued to watch the confessional booth. After a few moments, the door began to open. The woman stepped out of the confessional. Evelyn caught a glimpse of her face. It was indeed Lily. The other door opened and out stepped a tall, lean man wearing a full white-collared shirt and black cassock. His face was pale, and he was firmly clutching his rosary as he was facing Lily. She took a step forward and leaned in on him. She went on her tiptoes and gave the pale priest a kiss on the cheek. After she regained her proper footing, the priest ran off toward the back of the sanctuary. Evelyn thought she heard the priest babble something in Latin as he ran. Lily wrapped the scarf around her neck once again and started toward the exit with an infatuated smirk.

"Run!"

"Wha?"

"Jesse, run!"

The statues of angels and saints watched as Evelyn and Jesse ran away from the church. They kept running, turned the street corner, and found a bookstore to hide in. Evelyn peered out the door's windows to see if Lily had noticed them.

"What did you see?" Jesse stuttered while he was catching his breath.

"Lily kissed the priest."

"All right, padre. Was it a full frontal lip-on-lip action kiss, or did it look like it was open mouth? I bet her tongue could do such amazing things."

Evelyn gave Jesse a cold stare. "Why would she kiss the priest?"

"Maybe she's been a bad girl."

"Get your mind out of the gutter. Anyway, that wouldn't explain why the priest would take off after she kissed him. With her allure, any man, religious or not, would jump at the chance."

"You can say that again."

Another cold stare went Jesse's way. He placed his right palm behind his head.

"So she's a little promiscuous. What does it matter? The priest running away is simply because of the devotion to God. Celibacy must be such a bitch."

"He was really pale and clutching something in his hand though."

Jesse said nothing.

Evelyn began thinking aloud. "She doesn't like religious officials or church, yet she goes to confession. She believes in love, yet she's ditching Seth for a priest. And I just remembered something else. She's still married. She keeps mentioning this husband of hers, but I've never heard a name dropped. Have you?"

Jesse shook his head back and forth. "Now that you mention it, no, I haven't."

"Then what's the deal? Something just doesn't feel right here."

Jesse rolled his eyes. "Did you ever stop to think that maybe it's too painful for her to mention his name? She seems to really be in love with the guy, and the name may spark some depressing loss. To be perfectly fair, you don't really talk about your parents in any more of a way than she does of her husband."

"But they're dead."

"They're still lost to you."

She turned away from him. "Whatever Mr. Rational Cold and Calculating Science Man."

Jesse placed his hands on his hips and pointed his elbows outwards in pose. "When you say it that way, it makes me want to get a cape and traverse the city, righting wrongs and theological thoughts."

Evelyn turned to Jesse and noticed his pose. She had a smile on her face. "You're such a nob." She kissed him with an open mouth.

"Evey, you're making this out to be something that it isn't. It's just coincidence. She was just thanking the priest for clearing her conscious."

Her bright blue eyes looked into his chestnut-coloured ones. "I suppose you're right. She's a good girl, very open, welcoming, and becoming."

He embraced her. "Are you better now?"

"Yeah." Evelyn shook her head up and down. "I bet she's off to meet Seth now. She probably just had errands to run first. Forgive me for dragging you away?"

"Why should I? Your curiosity can be quite the loveable quirk."

Evelyn playfully shoved Jesse.

"What do you say that we go home?"

Evelyn agreed, and the two left the bookstore. The rain was continuing to pour.

Jesse laughed. "If I didn't know any better, I'd say we'd have a flood on our hands."

"If there were a flood," Evelyn said with a smile, "we could hop aboard and get married much quicker."

Jesse smirked and placed his right arm around her. They talked about wedding plans as they slowly made their way back to their car in the soothing rainfall.

Seven

Lily was in the nursery during her break. She was standing watch over the children, making sure they were doing all right and well taken care of. She slowly went from bassinet to bassinet, playing with those children who were awake. She would play such games like peek-a-boo or blow gently on their stomachs. With some, she would use her fingers to tickle the bottom of their small feet. All of her actions resulted in the child's laughter and undivided attention toward her. The back door of the nursery opened. The matronly Tamara walked in.

"Hi, Lily. I see that you're enjoying your break."

"Sure am. I can never get enough of them." She made some gurgling baby noises down toward her current enchanted before she looked up and over at Tamara. She noticed something in her hands. "What is that you've got there?"

"A necklace," Tamara said, "although it seems more like an amulet. The Katz are highly superstitious and asked that we place it on their son right away."

Lily's right eye twitched. "Don't you think it's a little premature to be placing an amulet around a child who's not even a couple days old? He could place it in his mouth and choke on it or something."

Tamara heaved a sigh. "I hear your concern, but their son is not ready to leave our care. They would have pulled him if we didn't agree, so we had no choice but to comply."

Shaken, Lily spoke. "Well, it is good that we make sure he is properly taken care of. That is why we got into this field after all."

"Exactly. Plus, you spend a lot of time in here so we know we have someone to watch him in case he does attempt to swallow the pendant."

Lily answered with reluctance in her voice. "This is true."

"Say, Lily, can you do me a favour?" Lily listened. "As you're closer to him than I am and seeing how I have to get back to work, how about you place it on him?"

Tamara threw the necklace over to Lily, who caught it with her right hand. She looked down at the necklace dangling in her fingers and noticed three names inscribed on it. All three names started with S. The emerald became suddenly erratic as the necklace graciously fell from her anxious hands and onto the floor.

"Are you all right?"

"I'm sorry, Tamara. I can't have any part in this." She skittishly took off toward the door. "I just can't believe that parents would jeopardize their child in this way."

Lily left the nursery. Tamara walked over to the Katz's bassinet and kneeled down to pick up the amulet. She looked at it and then to the doorway. She turned around and noticed Lily hastily passing by the glass wall. She gave her a good look, looked back down at the necklace in her hands, and turned it over, noticing the names. She turned and looked at the Katz's son. Some uneasy feeling caused her to shudder.

"No, it couldn't be."

Lily bumped into Evelyn as she turned around the corner just past the glass wall on her way to the elevator. Evelyn noticed she was troubled.

"Are you okay? You look upset about something."

"You know the Katz baby?" She did not give Evelyn a chance to answer. "The parents are jeopardizing the well-being of their son."

"And they're doing this how?"

The emerald was blazing with seething anger. "They threatened to take him out of our care prematurely if they couldn't place a necklace around him. A necklace! Do you believe it? The child could choke on it for Christ's sake!"

Evelyn placed her hands on Lily's shoulders. "Lily, calm down."

Lily moved out from under Evelyn's hands. "How can I be calm when, at any possible second, the child can choke to death? I can't always be in there making sure he doesn't. I'm not on break 24/7." She hastily resumed on her course to the elevator.

"Where are you going?" Evelyn said as she followed her.

"Outside to have a smoke. I can't stand to think about this. It makes my blood boil."

Lily pressed the button for the elevator. When it didn't open right away, she kept pressing the button. Evelyn came up closer behind her.

"Lily, don't worry. We can put a chair in front of the window and have Bruce or Ryan keep watch over him or something."

She stopped pressing the button and turned to Evelyn. "A vigil. That makes me feel a little better."

"Nothing will happen to that child," Evelyn reassured her, "especially when you're on watch."

Lily's eyes shifted toward the ground. "I'm not so sure if I can go back in there until he's gone."

Evelyn seemed confused.

"I have this feeling that, every time I'll look at him, I'll become instantly unnerved and pissed off. It wouldn't be fair to the others who are in the nursery. I'll be happy when he's gone home, as long as I don't read about an infanticide in the paper."

Lily's eyes shifted up and over Evelyn's right shoulder and forward. She noticed Tamara, who was giving her an odd glance from down the hallway. The emerald focused sharply. Her eyes swung back to Evelyn. "I still need that cigarette. Are you busy at the moment?"

"Actually, Tamara has me looking at the stock of supplies. Can you wait about fifteen minutes 'til I'm on break?"

"My break ends in twenty, but, after my smoke, I'll be in the cafeteria for a very quick bite. If you want a really quick chat, you know where to find me."

"Okay."

The elevator made its standard pinging noise, and the doors opened. Lily stepped through and pressed the button for the main floor. She kept her eyes on Tamara in the background as the doors closed in front of her.

Eight

Evelyn walked into the locker room. She noticed Lily sitting on the benches. Her eyes were red and puffy, and her face seemed slightly stained. She rushed over and sat next to her. "Oh my God. Lily, are you okay?"

Lily regained her composure. "Oh, hi, Evelyn." She sniffled. "I'll be all right."

"What happened?"

Lily wiped the corner of her eyes. "I guess you could say that I'm single again."

Evelyn embraced her. "When did all of this happen?"

"A few days ago." Lily wiped her nose.

"What went wrong? Last I saw, you two seemed perfectly fine together."

She shook her head slowly from side to side and laughed. "My effect kicked in."

Evelyn tilted her head sideways. "How do you mean?"

"You saw him. He was becoming attached to my hip. Slowly at first, but it quickly escalated. It only became worse from that day he came to this floor to pick me up."

Evelyn placed her hands on top of Lily's. "What brought all of this on?"

"I was making dinner for the two of us. It was nothing overly special or different, but, after we sat down to eat, he asked me to marry him."

"And you told him no?"

"Well, what else could I say? You know I'm still married. I'm not a bloody polygamist. One marriage at a time, and one marriage only. "

"Did you tell him that?"

Lily nodded her head up and down.

"And how'd he take it?"

She told Evelyn that he didn't take it so well. Her eyes wandered about the room. "It's not like my husband would be coming home anytime soon, and I stressed this to him. I told him how we could continue carrying on how we had been, but it didn't work. I think he felt used and thought that, no matter what I said, I never took it seriously. He started asking me if there was anything he could do to prove to me that he was in love with me. After that, he stormed off."

"Where do you think he went?"

Lily's right hand gave motion away from her body. "I have no idea. Maybe to think? But that was five days ago. I went to the Ivy yesterday to talk with him, hoping he cooled down. When I asked for him, the hostess said he just up and quit three days prior. I asked some of his friends at work how he was doing, and they had no idea either. They said that, when they tried to call him, there was no answer. I decided to try his flat next, but, when I arrived, there were no lights on. I must have knocked on that door for a good ten minutes before I left. It's almost as if he just vanished."

Evelyn had some worry in her voice. "Do you think he did anything to himself?"

Lily stood up and made her way to her locker. Her back was to Evelyn as she opened the locker doors. "I wouldn't think so. I've seen this happen time and time again. He's probably taking some of my words to him to heart and figuring out a way to prove his worth. That's usually the way it goes."

"You should hire a bodyguard or something just in case Seth is stalking you."

Lily smirked as she reached for her change of clothes. "I can handle the crazy," she confidently told Evelyn. "I've talked with Bruce and Ryan, and they're on alert for him just in case he decides to show up here and pull some sort of scene."

"Do you think he would?"

"Not sure. But, sooner or later, they always turn up in some form or another." The emerald shone as she placed her back against her locker. "I know this is going to sound a little crazy, but, in his begging, I saw an undisputable glimmer of passion in him. It was pure and innocent and without pretext."

Lily seemed to drift off.

Evelyn looked perplexed. "You're right. That does sound crazy."

Lily laughed. "I sure know how to pick them, don't I?"

"What are you going to do now?"

"It depends on what he does next."

"You're going to hold out for him?"

"For a little while. He's earned the right."

Evelyn did not know what to say.

"I know how weird I must sound, considering Seth seems to have gone off the deep end, but love can be quite the delusional extremity."

Evelyn gave a blank stare.

"An ecliptic liturgy as it were."

Evelyn continued to stare blankly at Lily. She looked over and noticed Evelyn's empty gaze.

"What?"

"I think I'm going to have to start carrying around a dictionary with me."

Lily quietly laughed. The door to the locker room opened. Both girls looked over to see who had entered. It was Ms. Fraystl. She seemed somewhat anxious.

"Have either of you two seen or heard from Tamara lately?"

Evelyn and Lily looked at each other before answering. "Not for a couple days."

"Is something the matter?" Evelyn asked.

Ms. Fraystl sighed. "She hasn't been to work in three days, and no one else has heard from her. I'm starting to worry. It's not like her to not call in if she isn't going to make it. Last time anyone saw her was when Bruce was on the night shift four days ago."

Evelyn had a look of worry in her face. "I thought she was sick or out on vacation."

"No," replied Ms. Fraystl. "Bruce said she was acting odd as well. In all of his twenty-two years that he's known her, he said he's never seen her act like that."

"Like what?" asked Lily.

"She seemed distracted. It was as if she had a haunting thought and this place just didn't seem like a home to her anymore. His words, not mine."

"When did all of this start?" Evelyn worriedly asked.

"Somewhere around a week ago. Apparently, it was getting progressively worse. Did she say anything to either of you?"

Evelyn and Lily looked at each other and then to Ms. Fraystl.

Lily spoke first. "Last time I had an actual conversation with her, we were in the nursery, and she seemed perfectly normal."

Evelyn just shook her head from side to side to let Ms. Fraystl know she knew nothing.

Ms. Fraystl looked back toward Lily. "What did you two talk about?"

"Just about the Katz's parents pushing and threatening to take him out of here if we didn't place the necklace around his neck."

Ms. Fraystl exhaled heavily. "Oh God, that rigmarole. What a pain in the side those parents were."

Lily nodded in agreement as she recollected the events to Ms. Fraystl. "Tamara agreed with me that it wasn't such a good idea. Nothing peculiar happened before I stormed off because of the parents' atrocity toward their son. I waved to her when I saw her next, but, because of our schedules, we didn't have a chance to really talk. She seemed chipper as always."

"Did you call her husband?" Evelyn solemnly interjected. "Does he know anything?"

"He's as much in the dark about this as we are. All we know is that she left the hospital that early morning and never made it home."

Evelyn hurriedly followed up by asking Ms. Fraystl if anyone was doing anything to find her.

"We're filing a missing person's report. Beyond that and actually going out to find her ourselves, there's not much more we can do."

Evelyn's bright blue eyes sank toward the ground. Ms. Fraystl looked at both young women. "I know that now isn't really the time for this, but, because no one knows where on God's green earth she is, I have to temporarily appoint a new head nurse for this floor." She looked directly at Evelyn and then to Lily. "Lily, do you want the job?"

Lily had this very surprised look on her face. "I'd love to, but don't you think someone with more seniority should take over in Tamara's absence?"

"You're the most qualified for the job."

"All right then. It's just—"

She did not allow Lily to finish. "You'll start taking over her duties tomorrow if she doesn't show up."

Ms. Fraystl turned and left the locker room. Evelyn leaned over and gave Lily a somewhat hesitant hug. "Congratulations."

"Thanks. I guess."

"It's a big opportunity."

"I suppose. It should at least keep my mind off this whole Seth thing for the next little while." She noticed some anguish in Evelyn's bright blue eyes. "Are you okay?"

Evelyn looked around. "Ya. I couldn't take those extra hours anyway."

"Not about the job, sweetie. About Tamara."

"I'll be okay."

The emerald began to scan Evelyn. "Tamara didn't act peculiar toward you in the past few days, did she?"

Evelyn shook her head no. "We just talked about wedding stuff. Nothing was out of the ordinary. Like you said, she was chipper as always."

Lily ran her hand softly down Evelyn's arm. "What do you say about us going to talk to Bruce?"

"I think I want to see Jesse first."

"Sure. Come, I'll walk you to the stairwell."

The two left the locker room and started making their way over to the nurses' station. It was silent all the way. Once they arrived, Evelyn and Lily broke off from each other. Lily approached Bruce as Evelyn was still heading toward the stairwell.

"Hi, Bruce."

He acknowledged her with a slight gesture of his hand. "Hey, Lily. Still no sign of your ex-boyfriend."

"Okay, but that's not what brings me here."

Bruce curiously looked at her.

"We just found out about Tamara." The emerald watched him closely. "You've worked with her for a long time. If she were acting strangely, I think you would be one of the first people she'd talk to. Did she happen to say anything peculiar to you before her disappearance?"

"All that I know, I told Ms. Fraystl."

Lily took a step closer to him. "Think, Bruce. Think."

Bruce scratched the back of his head. "Give me a minute."

As she continued to talk with Bruce, Evelyn made her way into the stairwell. She walked up to the children's floor and began to search for Jesse. She fell into his arms once she found him.

"Whoa, Evey. What's wrong?"

"Tamara's missing."

Jesse was shocked. "What?"

"We just found out. No one has seen her for four days."

Jesse placed his arms around her. He filled a paper cup with water and took Evelyn over to an empty room, where they sat on a bed. "What happened?"

"No one knows." Evelyn drank her water. "All we know is that she left for home four days ago and Bruce was the last to see her. Ms. Fraystl says that, according to her husband, Tamara never even made it home."

Jesse took the empty paper cup out of Evelyn's hands. "Does Bruce know anything else?"

She shook her head from side to side. "Not sure. As I was leaving to come see you, Lily was questioning him on it."

Evelyn curled into Jesse. He stroked her hair. "All that has been done to find her is a filed missing person's report."

"I'm sure everything will be fine, Evey. She'll be found and be better than ever in time for the wedding. Don't you worry, buckaroo."

Evelyn looked up at him. "I hope you're right."

Jesse looked into her bright blue eyes. Something else seemed off to him. "It seems like there's something else on your mind besides Tamara. Anything you want to talk about?"

She exhaled heavily. "Because Tamara is missing, Ms. Fraystl promoted Lily to head nurse of the ward. She said Lily was the most qualified for the job."

"And this bothers you?" He continued to stroke her hair.

"Of course it does. I mean, I wouldn't have taken the job in any event, but I wasn't even considered for it."

"Did Lily openly accept it?"

"Not really. She suggested that perhaps someone with more seniority should have the job instead, but Fraystl just ignored her."

Jesse pondered for a second or two. "It's probably because she spends a lot of her free time in the nursery. Fraystl probably noticed it, and that's why she offered it to Lily. Because of the hard work and initiative."

Evelyn sat up. "Are you saying that I'm not a hard worker?"

"I'm not saying that."

"Then what exactly are you saying?"

Jesse took a moment to choose his words. "All I'm saying is that she's a harder worker than you are. Hell, she's a harder worker than I am and most everyone else here at this hospital. The doctors here should take a page from her book of work ethic."

She laid back into his arms. "That's another thing," she began thinking aloud again. "Why does she even work at all? She can do anything she wants to."

Jesse gave it a moment. "Maybe she doesn't like having all that free time. Maybe she just likes to interact with people, or maybe it's like she's said. She likes being around children."

Evelyn sat up again, but now gave Jesse a cold stare. "Are you defending her?"

He put his arms up to his chest and shook his wrists back and forth. "How can I be defending her when there's nothing to defend her from?"

"Why don't you try defending me for a change instead of attacking?"

Jesse was confounded. "How am I attacking you?" He gazed past her cold stare. "This isn't about the job or Lily, is it?"

Evelyn's bright blue eyes wandered to her right side.

"You're upset over Tamara because you fear the worst. You don't want to lose another mother figure. Is that it?"

Evelyn's eyes filled with tears.

Jesse poked her on the nose. "Don't you worry, buckaroo."

Evelyn didn't smile. Jesse kissed the top of her head. "I think I should take you home." Evelyn put up a small fight. "Why should I go home? You think I'm not stable enough to continue working?"

"Well-"

"Well what?"

He looked in her bright blue eyes. "You're in no condition to work. Are you hesitant because you just don't want to talk to Fraystl?"

Evelyn did not respond.

"Fine then," he said. "Go change, and I'll talk with her."

"You sure?"

"Positive."

The two stood up from the bed, made their way out of the empty room, and walked silently all the way toward the stairwell. When they reached Evelyn's floor, they saw Lily still talking with Bruce. Ms Fraystl was there now as well. Lily looked over when she heard the door close and noticed the swollen and sombre look on Evelyn's face. She turned and started talking to Ms. Fraystl. Evelyn passed the assembly and walked down the halls as Jesse made his way toward the small crowd.

"Hate to bother you, but—"

"It's okay, Jesse," Ms. Fraystl said. "You can take Evelyn home."

Jesse looked confused. "How'd you know I was going to ask that?"

"Lily just spoke on your behalf."

He turned his head to Lily and then back to Ms. Fraystl "You're sure this is okay?"

Ms. Fraystl nodded. "With everything that's going on right now, I don't blame her for wanting to go home early. If my matron of honour was missing, I'd want to be at home myself."

"Thanks."

Lily took Jesse by the arm and led him away from the gathered pack. "How's she holding up?"

"She's all over the place. Any new developments on this end?"

Lily sighed. "Bruce is a bloody twit. Either he actually doesn't have a memory or he knows more than he's letting on. In any event, I don't trust him."

"You think he may have something to do with all of this?"

She shook her head from side to side. "Not sure, but it's fairly suspicious that the last person to see her has a very small recollection of the event, especially when they've worked together for the past twenty-two years, don't you think?"

Jesse didn't even need to think of it after Lily's accusation. "That does make sense."

"He seems unstable with all of this, but is trying to hide it. And where was Ryan? He was scheduled to be on duty that night as well. I even waved good-bye to him as I left. It would have been very convenient for him to be in the washroom or grabbing a bite as she was leaving."

Jesse rubbed his chin. "You think the two are in cahoots?"

"It's possible."

"But?"

"It just doesn't make sense. Why now after all these years? Bruce has known her for twenty-two years, and Ryan has known her for nine."

"So where are you heading with this now?"

"I'm going to ask about and subtly imply Ryan to see if there is any reaction."

Jesse glanced over at Bruce. "Sounds interesting. You'll have to let me know of anything when I come back tonight."

Lily raised an eyebrow. "You're just going to take Evelyn home and then come back to work?"

"Is something wrong with that?"

"I wouldn't recommend it."

He looked away from Bruce and focused his chestnut eyes on Lily. "And why is this?"

She rolled her eyes. "She's very emotional now, right? Do you really want her starting a fight with you that will start off with something to the effect of abandoning her in her time of need?"

Jesse said nothing.

"She may even go into how if this is how it is now then what'll happen once we're married."

"I never thought of it that way before. You think she will?"

Lily took him a little further away from the assembled. She looked left and right for Evelyn.

"Look, Jesse, I'm not supposed to tell you this, but she's iffy on the marriage thing."

Jesse was shocked at this news. "What?"

Lily put up her right hand. "Don't misunderstand. She does want to marry you, but she's just worried that, after it happens and the honeymooning settles down, it'll all be downhill from there. It would be wise if you just stayed away tonight. I'll handle this. If I get any new information, I will fill you two in. Don't you worry."

Jesse seemed as if he were about to become lost. "She really said that?"

"Not in so many words, but you can't let this eat away at you. She does want to be Mrs. Jesse Chamberlain. That much is certain, but that's not the issue." He looked at her. "The issue is this Tamara thing. Don't make it out to be something that it's not."

"I suppose."

The emerald flickered. "Don't suppose. Do it."

"Okay, okay. You make total sense. I'm not arguing that. I'll stay home with her tonight and comfort her to no end."

"That's a good, understanding boy."

"Why do I have this feeling that I'm going to owe you one big time?"

"Perhaps because, deep down inside, you know I'm always right."

"That could be it." He grinned.

Lily shook her head. "You're such a goof at times."

"It's part of my charm."

Lily rolled her eyes. "Uh-huh. Just make sure that charm of yours doesn't interfere with tonight. Remember, this is for her."

"I understand." Jesse nodded his head up and down.

Lily looked over and noticed Evelyn and her change of clothes coming down the hall. She ran her hand down Jesse's arm and went back over to Bruce and Ms. Fraystl. Evelyn continued down the hallway until she met up with Jesse.

"Do you have everything?"

"Everything I need," Evelyn replied.

They turned and walked a few feet. Evelyn pressed the button for the elevator. They both heard Lily continuing to question Bruce and Ms. Fraystl about that night and Ryan. The elevator made its standard pinging noise, and the doors opened. They walked in, and Evelyn hit the button for the main floor. The elevator closed its doors. Down to the main floor they went.

"What is the questioning of Ryan all about?" Evelyn asked while staring at the elevator doors.

Jesse looked down and to his right. "She thinks either Bruce or Ryan is involved in this."

"How is that?"

Jesse filled her in on Lily's suspicions about Bruce and Ryan.

"So she's still on the case?"

"You know her. She's an inquisitor. There won't be anyone left in her path when she gets to the bottom of this."

"That's good. We need to find Tamara and see if anything has happened to her." She formed a fist with her right hand "The person or persons involved need to pay. I think Lily will make sure of that, don't you?"

"Definitely."

The elevator pinged to let the couple know they were on the main floor. The doors opened, and they departed from it. They walked silently past the circular reception desk and the rest of the mock granite-coloured halls until they reached their car.

"Evey?"

"Yes?"

"Are you sure you're okay with all of these current events that are going on?"

"I'm fine really."

"Okay then," he said as his voice trailed with some uncertainty.

He opened the door for Evelyn and then jumped into the driver's side seat. Before he started the engine, he placed his right hand over Evelyn's left. She took her hand out from under his and placed it on top of her right hand, which was resting in her lap as she stared blankly out the window. He was going to say something, but decided against it. He reluctantly started the engine for the drive home.

Nine

Lily and Evelyn were making their way back from the cafeteria after a mediocre, sandwich-filled dinner. Just before they reached the circular reception desk on the main floor, they heard a commotion of shouts and sirens from the outside beyond the automatic doors of the hospital. They quickly hurried over to see what was transpiring. The doors opened accompanied by a paramedic, nurses, and a now-stained gurney.

"We need to get her to the OR!" shouted the paramedic.

Evelyn and Lily watched as the nurses were quickly making their way toward them. As they passed by, Evelyn became horrified as she recognized the bloodstained and heavily cut face. She ran down to catch up with the gurney.

"What happened here?"

"Miss, please, stay back," the paramedic said. "We need to get her to surgery ASAP."

"See this smock?" Evelyn furiously said. "It means I work here, so don't you fucking tell me what to do, paramedic boy! I need to know what happened to her!"

Evelyn was hearing words from the nurses as she ran with the gurney, but all the medical jargon melded together. The only thing she was able to make out was the paramedic telling her that an officer would fill her in on the details before he pushed her away. She watched in terror as the gurney pushed past the silver-coloured swinging doors of the operating room. She fell to her knees. She held her stomach with her right arm as she hunched forward. Her left arm was straight, and her palm was flush to the floor, supporting her.

Lily came rushing down the hallway. She stopped in the middle and dropped to her knees. She put her arms around a shaking Evelyn and called her name.

It took a couple times, but, when she finally heard Lily calling her name, she asked, "Do you see a police officer anywhere?" Lily turned her head to look down the hallway toward the automatic doors. "One just came in."

"Can you help me up?"

Lily placed her right arm around her back and positioned her head under Evelyn's left shoulder and rose.

"Okay, I think I can walk."

Lily let her go slowly. After a stumble or two, Evelyn was standing fine. She started to make her way down the corridor toward the officer. Lily walked with her just in case.

"What the fuck happened?" she said as she stormed toward the officer.

"Excuse me, miss?"

"What do you think I'm talking about? The bloody weather? The woman who was just rushed into the OR. What fucking happened to her?"

Lily rubbed the middle of Evelyn's back with her right hand. "You'll have to excuse her, officer. We work with that woman on our ward. She is her matron of honour, so if you could—"

The officer looked at Evelyn and bowed his head. The emerald flashed as she observed him.

"We received an anonymous tip on the whereabouts of a missing person, so we decided to check the location. When my partner and I arrived at the scene, we noticed the windows were boarded up. We knocked on the doors, but there was no answer. It looked a little suspicious so we decided to enter the premises. The house was empty, and we were going to leave until we found the basement door."

"I didn't ask for the details," Evelyn impatiently said. "Get to the bloody point."

"We opened the door and proceeded down the curved concrete stairwell. This thick, coppery smell was in the air. As we were nearing the end of the stairs, we saw this woman tied to a chair at the far end of the room. We stopped and looked at the floor. Blood reached from where she was tied to near close the end of the stairs." The officer took in a breath as if he was trying to forget the scene. "It wasn't exactly fresh. It was more like a viscous residue. She wasn't moving, but, when my partner checked her pulse, he said it was faint, but still there. He was telling me that, from the looks of it, she must have been tortured for days. We got on the radio and immediately called for an ambulance."

Evelyn exploded. "Do you know the fucker who did this?"

The officer shook his head no. "There was no ID on him, and the house was abandoned to begin with."

Evelyn tilted her head slightly to the right. "What do you mean there was no ID on him? You caught him! Where is he now? I want to give that motherfucker a piece of my mind!"

"Another ambulance is on its way. It should be here shortly."

"Don't tell me you're going to try to save his life!"

"Well, not exactly, miss. I was watching the stairs to make sure no one could come in from behind as my partner was untying her. We heard someone else breathing, so we both turned around. We saw this man with a piece of glass in his hand hanging at his side. I swear he wasn't down there a moment ago. He was just standing there, breathing not more than ten feet in front of my partner. We were both yelling at him to drop the weapon, but he just continued to stand there, breathing very contently until he suddenly raised his hand and leapt. My partner instinctively reacted by firing a round at close range. He was dead before he hit the floor."

Evelyn's face lit up. "Fantastic!"

They heard the back doors of a vehicle close. Evelyn looked at the automatic doors. A gurney with a body bag entered through them. The paramedic was pushing his way past the officer.

"Stop," the officer said to the paramedic. "These two here work with the victim. Maybe they might know who this guy is. Just show his face. The rest is too unbearable for even me to see again."

The paramedic sighed with his eyes, but nodded toward the police officer and unzipped the top of the body bag. He pulled the bag backwards, exposing the top of the shoulders and the face of the torturer. Lily placed her hands over her mouth and started to gag. Evelyn stood dumbfounded when she saw his face.

"Do you know him?" the officer asked.

Evelyn was still in dead stare. Lily removed her hands from her mouth and took a deep breath. "His name is Seth Kirkpatrick."

The officer took out a pad of paper and a pen. "Did he work here as well?"

"No."

"Then how do you know the perpetrator?"

"We used to date." Lily wrapped her arms around herself. "We broke up, and he just disappeared. He up and quit his job. No one could reach him. We just thought he was depressed."

Evelyn and Lily heard the sound of the stairwell door closing. They looked up and saw Jesse running down the hallway toward them. When he reached the gurney, he stood in between Lily and Evelyn.

"What's going on? I just heard that Tamara is fighting for her life in the OR." He looked down at the gurney. "Holy shit! What the fuck happened?"

Lily looked over at Jesse. She summed up the officer's words for him. Jesse placed his right hand on his forehead. "Christ!" He placed his arms around Lily. "Are you okay?"

"I have no idea."

Jesse leaned back. The officer interrupted this grisly reunion the quartet seemed to be having by telling the paramedic to zip up the body bag. He did so, and both he and the officer began to make their way to the morgue until Lily stopped them.

"If you want, I can go with you and give any further information I know so you can wrap this up."

The officer nodded. The three continued toward the morgue.

"Evey, sweetie," Jesse said.

Evelyn was staring forward without blinking.

"Hey, buckaroo." He snapped his fingers in front of her face. "Are you in there?"

Evelyn collapsed. She had fainted.

"Someone!" he shouted as he picked her up. "Anyone! Help me!"

He found a doctor with the help of the receptionist at the circular desk. They brought Evelyn to an examination room, where the doctor began examining her on the plush examination table.

"So Doc, what's the prognosis?"

The doctor used his pen flashlight as he opened Evelyn's eyes with his left hand. "You said she just collapsed?"

"Yeah."

"She seems fine. It's most likely an anxiety attack. Is she on any medication?"

"No."

"Is this the first time or has it happened before?"

"It's the first time I know of."

"Is she going through a stressful time?"

"Well, a missing co-worker of hers who is to be her matron of honour was just admitted to the OR after being tortured by someone we know."

"That could do it." The doctor moved to the door. "Just let her get some rest, and she'll be fine when she wakes up."

Jesse kissed her hand and walked out of the examination room. He began to make his way over to the morgue. He noticed the officer and paramedic walking away as he was making his way closer. He arrived at the door and looked through the rectangular glass piece found in the upper right side. Lily was at the head end of a cold slab. He watched her as she leant forward and kissed Seth's forehead. He opened the door. She turned around.

"So Seth is the one responsible for this whole thing?"

"It would appear so."

"How did he even know who Tamara was?"

Lily placed her right index finger under her nose while she rested her thumb underneath her chin. "I've been thinking about that myself." She took a second. "I think it was that time he came to pick me up on the floor instead of waiting for me in the cafeteria. That's probably when he noticed her, which means he saw everyone else that I worked with." She took a deep breath and lowered her arm. "I'm just glad he was stopped before he did anything to anyone else." She looked down and placed her right palm over Seth's closed eyes.

"Any idea why he did this?"

She began to walk down the slab. Her hand was slowly running down Seth's side. "My best guess would be that, because he couldn't have me all to himself, he'd hurt those around me in order to have it."

"Is there any news on Tamara's condition?"

"Last I heard, she was still in surgery."

"Do you think she'll be okay?"

Lily shook her head slowly from side to side in grief. "No idea. The officer said it didn't look good considering the length of the torture." She took her hand off Seth. She looked up and over to Jesse, who was now standing next to her at the end of the slab.

"How's Evelyn doing?"

He breathed deeply through his nostrils. "She blacked out."

"Is she all right?"

"She's fine. A doctor said she had a panic attack or was in shock or something like that. She's resting now."

Lily looked back at Seth. "Poor Evelyn."

"How are you holding up?"

Lily leaned into Jesse and grasped his hand. "I've been better, but I think I'll be fine." She looked up at him, and his eyes locked in hers. "It's going to be a long night." She let go of his hand. "If you wouldn't mind, I'd like some time alone to talk with him before I head over to the observatory over the OR."

Jesse looked down at the corpse and then to Lily. "Sure."

He turned around and walked to the door. As he was leaving, he briefly turned back and saw Lily talking to her dead lover. He hung his head, sighed, pushed the door forward, and left the morgue.

Ten

Evelyn inhaled heavily. "I can't go through with this. I hate the fourth floor of this hospital. I vowed never to come back to it after Father died."

Jesse pressed the button for the elevator. "Come now, Evey. Don't you think that Tamara would appreciate your visit?"

Evelyn turned to her left and faced him. "She's in a coma and still in critical condition. I don't think she appreciates much of anything at the moment." She turned back to the elevator doors. "Even if our little visit sparks something in her, she'll never leave the floor. That's why it's called long-term care. The only people who get to leave are those of us who are left behind."

The elevator pinged, and the doors opened. They stepped inside. Jesse pushed the button for the fourth floor. The elevator started to rise after it closed its doors.

"You'll be fine. I'm here with you. Plus, you have Lily to talk to when you're working. You have a support group."

"I guess."

Jesse looked down to his right at her. "I know the last couple days have been hectic and we haven't talked about it, but you don't blame her for this, do you?"

"It was her boyfriend who did all of this."

"But I seem to recall you insinuating that she should go for him at the restaurant despite what she said about her effect."

"This isn't my fault."

"I know that, and neither is it hers. I realize you're in a bad place right now, but do you really think that she could be held accountable for his actions? It's not her fault that he tried to prove his love for her in such a way."

The numbered lights above the doors stopped, and the doors opened. Evelyn nervously walked through first. Jesse followed closely behind her.

"I know that. Don't confuse this with anything else. I forgot how you can so logically rationalize everything to such a degree, but you've never lost a mother before, let alone two, so don't try to pretend like you know anything that is going on inside of my head."

They walked the rest of the way silently to Tamara's private room. Evelyn entered first and saw Tamara motionless in the bed with many tubes coming out of her. She held back a whimper. Lily was standing on the far side of the bed with Tamara's stout-looking, grey-bearded husband, the rabbi. They were both looking down at Tamara as they were talking. She made her way over to the other side of the bed. She looked down at Tamara herself.

"Any change?"

The rabbi shook his head from side to side. Evelyn walked over and hugged him.

"How are you, Evelyn?" She breathed a heavy breath. "I just don't know anymore, rabbi. This all just seems like a bad dream that I can't wake up from. How about you?"

"More or less the same, although Lily here has been kind enough to keep me company through these past couple days."

Lily looked over to the rabbi. "It's the least I could do."

He placed his big hand on top of hers, which was resting on the side protectors of the bed. "It's still greatly appreciated."

The emerald shimmered.

"What's next?" Evelyn asked. "There must be something that we can do."

The rabbi looked over to Evelyn. "We hope she is able to come out of this coma. There's not much else."

A few tears dribbled down Evelyn's face. The room was silent with the exception of Evelyn's tears staining the floor and the noises of the machines attached to Tamara.

"I never did get the chance to congratulate you two on getting engaged." The rabbi looked at Evelyn and Jesse. "I do have one question for you though."

Jesse and Evelyn listened.

"Are you sure you don't wish to be married by an ordained minister of any sort of faith?"

Evelyn and Jesse looked at each other. Jesse answered for the both of them. "Well, rabbi, we're kind of faithless people."

"You honestly believe that something greater than us isn't at work here?"

Lily could not help but smirk. No one happened to notice this.

Evelyn did not understand the rabbi's words. "You honestly still have faith at a time like this? Look what's happened to your wife."

Lily's eyes were shifting back and forth between Evelyn and the rabbi. The emerald was keeping close watch.

"Faith," the rabbi said, "like marriage, is a beautiful thing, but it requires much work. There isn't really any skill involved with it. It's a constant tide of ebb and flow. One just needs to make sure that the current does not overtake them and send them to the bottom of the ocean."

Evelyn did not know what to say.

"If you believe in it, for better or worse, it'll all work out in the end."

Lily noticed Evelyn's bright blue eyes were beginning to slouch. Jesse was holding onto her and moving his head closer in order to rest it on her neck, trying to hide the fact that he could not directly look at the rabbi.

"You may not have known it, but Tamara would go on about you two crazy kids. Even though we could not conceive, in some way, I always thought she saw you as the daughter we never had."

Evelyn fought back some tears.

"She was honoured to be your matron."

"I'm the one who should be honoured." Evelyn looked down at Tamara. "I feel as if it would have been a great blessing to have someone who has been married for as long as you two to be standing by my side." She took her hand and passed it through Tamara's thin, grey hair. "Guess that won't be happening anymore."

The emerald quickly lit up. "I have an idea."

All three looked at her.

"Why don't you ordain them, rabbi?"

Evelyn interjected.

"Don't worry, Evelyn," Lily said. "Neither of you are Jewish, so it wouldn't be official or able to be upheld in any court of man for that matter. We'll do it to what you're most aware of, which is Christian. He'll just ask you if you take Jesse and vice versa." She moved her right hand sideways in front of her chest back and forth a couple of times. "We'll keep the 'So help you God' part right out. Just to be safe, we'll leave out anything with the word 'lawful' in it, too. I'll act as witness, and Tamara can still be your matron of honour. This way, I can still be present, as you originally intended."

Jesse looked at Evelyn. "It is everything you've wanted, Evey."

She turned to Jesse. "That it is. What do you think?"

"Things have been kind of crazy lately. Would it lift your spirits until the actual ceremony?"

"I don't see how it wouldn't."

"Well, then."

Lily turned her head toward the rabbi. "How about you, rabbi? You in?"

"This is highly unorthodox, but, if Tamara's presence will help two people in love, then I don't see why not." The rabbi looked to his wife and then back to Lily. "What did you have in mind that I should say? I don't really know how this type of proclamation goes."

The emerald sparkled. "Go with the typical church vows. Then just pronounce them ordained to be married."

"Sounds reasonable." The rabbi looked at the couple. "All right. Are you two ready for this?"

The couple held each other's hands and nodded in agreement.

The rabbi looked to Jesse first. "Do you, Jesse Chamberlain, take this woman, in sickness and health, for richer or for poorer, in respect and honour for the rest of your life?"

"I do."

"And do you, Evelyn Bryce, take this man, in sickness and health, for richer or for poorer, in respect and honour for the rest of your life?"

"I do."

"Then from the eyes of those who are here with you today, I pronounce you ordained and ready to be wed in any way you deem fit."

Jesse and Evelyn kissed.

Lily applauded. "Now was that so bad, you two?"

Evelyn was blushing. Jesse seemed as if he could not wipe the smile from his face. Evelyn reached her arms over the bed and grabbed Lily's hands. "Thank you, Lily. You always know how to turn a situation around."

Lily grinned. "It's what I do. Do you want me to find a glass for Jesse to step on?"

Evelyn laughed. "That's okay, hun. You've done more than enough already."

Lily smiled a modest smile.

"This goes without saying, but I know my Tamara is honoured to have been present at this event."

Evelyn hugged and kissed the rabbi on his right cheek. "I'm honoured she was, too."

She put her arm around the rabbi's back as he started to tear up. They both watched Tamara resting peacefully. Jesse stood alone on the other side of the bed, his hands firmly on the bedside railings. Silence reigned in the room until the beeping on one of the machines diverted from its standard, consistent noise. A nurse came running in and pushed Jesse out of his way. He checked the body and called in a code blue over the PA system. He began performing CPR while another nurse came running in with a defibrillator. Evelyn turned into the rabbi's chest and buried her face into him. The nurses placed the defibrillator's paddles onto Tamara's chest and began the charge.

Eleven

Evelyn woke up alone on the leather couch in her small apartment. Jesse had gone to work his shift at the hospital. It had been two days since Tamara's funeral, and Evelyn was taking a bereavement leave. She was hazily looking up in the dimly lit room at the ceiling, her eyes milked over in dead stare. The television was on from earlier. Despite the fact she was not paying any attention to it, it remained the only source of illumination within the room. She wiped the area around her lips with her arm. She was no longer sure if the residue was formed from her mouth or her eyes. She moved the palms of her hands and placed them over her eyes, rubbing them to alleviate the dry feeling.

Evelyn rolled over so she was now on her stomach. She was staring forward over the arms of the couch and into the kitchen. The sink was starting to overflow with dishes. Sitting up and placing her right palm on her forehead as she tilted her head downward toward the floor, she figured she should clean them. She scratched the back of her head and shuffled her hair quickly with her left hand. She stood up and did not bother to stretch. Quickly, she looked above the couch at the only family heirloom she had. The heirloom was a piece of art given to the family as a gift many years ago. The art displayed a linear perspective of a humanist scene. No one knew just exactly how old it was or how they came into possession of it, but they continued to pass it down the line since time immemorial. The artwork usually helped Evelyn through tough times by remembering her family, but it was of only small comfort tonight.

She walked away from the painting and began making her way over to the kitchen. Just as she walked past the oak coffee table that lay a few feet away from the couch, she banged into the corner of it with her left leg. The corners were sharp. As she was not wearing any pants, it left a cut small enough that allowed for a few trickles of blood. She did not feel it and kept moving toward the kitchen. Once inside, she turned on the light and took the dishes out of the sink, placing them on the counter. She closed the drain and began to run the water before placing her elbows on the small space in front of the sink, where she rested her arms and hunched forwards. She looked into the sink and began to watch the bubbles that were forming from the water under the tap's location as the basin filled. The sound of the water coming from the tap in front of her was interrupted as she placed her hand under it. She slowly moved her fingers back and forth while it dripped between them. She placed her hand up to her forehead and ran it down the center of her hair with her wet fingers. She did this a few more times so that it was out of her face. More bubbles began to form and took to the current, further engulfing the basin after she poured some dishwasher soap into the stream. She turned off the tap and moved it away so it was no longer hanging over the sink. She grabbed the plates, cups, utensils, and other dishes and placed them in the ocean, drowning them beneath the tide and allowing them to soak.

She turned around and walked a couple steps to the refrigerator. After opening the door, she reached in and took one of Jesse's lagers from the inside of the refrigerator doorway. She reached to the shelf that was installed next to the fridge for a bottle opener. After having a drink, she brought her head back to a normal level and held the glass bottle in her left hand as she looked for something to eat. She wanted something quick and simple, something that was ready and did not have to be made. The produce basket found in the bottom of the refrigerator held plums, peaches, oranges, apples, and pears, but none of these caught her eye, so she closed the section. She looked to the door and noticed some eggs. Even though it would have been quick to make them scrambled, she quickly dismissed it as she did not want to create more dishes. She noticed a jar of olives. Placing the opened lager on the highest shelf in the refrigerator, she opened the jar. After eating a few, she placed the lid back on the container and returned it to the door. Picking up the lager once more, she eyed what else the fridge had to offer. Nothing caught her eye so she stepped back, removing her back from the door. As the door closed, she walked back to the kitchen's entrance to see what the pantry had to offer, but, before she made it there, she stopped in front of the shelf next to the fridge. She placed her hand into the fruit bowl resting there and took a handful of grapes mixed with berries before continuing to the pantry. She began to eat the grapes one by one. As she was sliding open the door to the pantry, she heard the jingle for the late-night news from the television. She ignored it and took back another drink of lager. Her bright blue eyes moved about the pantry, and she noticed an open package of crackers. Leaving the package inside the pantry, she drew from it, slowly eating a few with her free hand. She looked around and saw some walnuts, pasta, sauce, condiments, rice, oatmeal, miscellaneous canned foods, and rice.

She sighed and closed the pantry. On her way back to the fridge, she placed the now-empty glass lager bottle on the shelf with the fruit bowl. Picking up the bottle opener once more, she opened the refrigerator. After opening another lager, she took another glance around inside. Nothing caught her eye the second time around, so she closed the door once more. She walked over to the wash basin. She placed the half-empty bottle of lager on the counter next to her. Grabbing the steel wool, she placed her hands inside the tiny ocean of ceramic, steel, and bubbles.

"The religious community is in shock today after the discovery of the body of Father Thomas Bradley."

Evelyn looked over toward the direction of the television set. She left the contained basin ocean and sat down on the couch in front of the set as the desk anchor was going live to the field reporter. "Father Bradley, seen here, was a prime example of—"

Evelyn looked hard at the picture. She recognized the priest's face from the file photo, but could not place her finger on it. Suddenly, she remembered where she had seen him. Her bright blue eyes widened. She could not believe it.

"He was found earlier today in his private chambers at St. George's by one Sister Lucia. In reports from her and other officials of the parish, Father Bradley had become increasingly distant over the past two to three weeks, constantly retiring to his chambers, sometimes not even coming out to perform service. Some say it was as if he had a constant haunting thought."

"Did anyone know the reason for this distraction?" The female reporter behind the desk asked.

The field reporter shook his head. "Unfortunately not. The door to his chambers was constantly locked, which, as parishioners have said, was very unlike him. They said he was a welcoming man, a man who would speak with them and shake hands with them as they would leave after mass."

The slim woman sitting behind the desk in a grey business suit asked the field reporter just how long ago Father Bradley had passed away.

"According to the coroner on scene, he has apparently been deceased for approximately five to six days."

"How did the priest die?"

"His wrists had been cut."

Evelyn was held captivated as she continued to watch.

"The cuts appear to be self-inflicted, but the manner in which they were made stands out, bringing the question of if he truly took his own life or if it was someone upset with the Church."

"How do you mean?"

"There was one vertical cut and one horizontal, which formed the sign of the cross on each wrist. A razor blade was found at the scene, but, if this was a murder, how did the suspect flee? There is only one way into and out of Father Bradley's chambers, and the door was locked from the inside. Further analysis of the wounds and the blade will determine if it was self-inflicted."

Showing concern for the religious community, the blonde anchor asked how the staff and parishioners were doing.

"They're puzzled. This was a man who sponsored many causes in the community, from helping the homeless to single mothers. He would hold raffles and fund-raisers in the community to raise money for these causes. This is truly—"

Evelyn picked up the remote and turned off the television. She stood up in the dim light from the kitchen's illumination that made its way into the darkened living room. Thoughts of Lily began surging through her head. It had to be more than a coincidence, considering the recent events that had been transpiring. She was sure of it, or so her mind made her believe. She hastily made her way to the bedroom and slipped on some pants and pulled a sweater over her small shirt that showed her midriff. She grabbed her keys and left the apartment.

Twelve

The elevator made its standard pinging noise as the doors opened. Evelyn stepped off the elevator and into an eerie silence. There was no noise at all, just a waking calm that awaited her. She called out, but her voice simply echoed throughout the halls. She began making her way through the waiting area, passing straight-backed chairs and tables while constantly moving her eyes from side to side. As she was passing by the nurses' station desk, she lowered her eyes. Her face became horrified. The bodies of Ms. Fraystl and Ryan were motionless on the floor in front of her just behind the desk. She knelt toward the ground and checked their pulses. They had none. Their necks had been snapped. She placed her hands over her mouth to prevent herself from screaming. A tear ran down her cheek as she started to shake. Still on her knees, she looked over and noticed the sidearm still fastened to Ryan's hip. She leaned forward and removed the pistol from its holster. She cocked the pistol and took off the safety before jumping back over the desk and into the hallway. Slowly, very slowly, she began to walk down the rectangular-shaped void of mock concrete. She came to a room and peered around the corner of the opened door. Another body was motionless in a bed with a pillow over her head. Her breathing increased heavily. She had no need to check it as she knew the woman was already dead. In fact, she knew anyone else on that floor was dead. She took a deep breath and continued, stepping forward as if it were the first time she had ever done so. She stopped before turning the corner to the glass viewing wall of the nursery. Something inside of her knew that Lily was in there, so she dropped to the floor and crawled under the glass section of the dividing wall. After making her way to the end of the hallway, she moved her head to her left and peeked around the corner.

Bruce was sitting motionless against the wall on the bloodstained floor. Evelyn made her way over and inspected the body. His throat was slashed. Her bright blue eyes moved down his arms and noticed a blade clutched in his right hand. Her bright blue eyes kept going, and she noticed his pistol was missing from its holster. She turned away from him and made her way to the doorway of the nursery. She saw Lily there with her back to the doorway.

"Lily!" Evelyn shouted.

She turned around. Lily was not in her nurse's smock. She was dressed in black heels, navy blue pinstriped pants, and a vest buttoned over a cream bustier. Her Knights Templars cross swayed back and forth and back again due to the momentum of her turn.

"What have you done?"

Lily smirked as she closed her eyes. "If you're referring to that mess out there, I didn't lift a finger. It was all Bruce's doing." She opened her eyes. "I think Tamara's death drove him off the edge, or maybe it was the haunting thought that Seth's death wasn't enough justice for him as he secretly harboured strong emotions for her. He kept suspecting Ryan as having a part in it. It ate away inside of him, driving him to kill everyone on this floor before taking his own life."

Evelyn had this look of extreme horror on her face. "Seth didn't coincidentally go after Tamara, did he?"

Lily smirked once more. "Seth was willing to do anything to have me. When I told him to take care of Tamara, he didn't question it in the slightest. I seriously thought he would have killed her by the time I placed that anonymous phone call to the authorities. It sort of complicated matters, but life is full of surprises."

Evelyn drew the pistol up from her side and placed one hand over the other. They were shaking uncontrollably. "Why, Tamara? Tell me! Why get Seth to kill her?"

Lily put her hands, palm side up, in front of her. "Whoa there, buckaroo." She stepped to the side and revealed Jesse gagged and tied to a straight-backed chair. "You don't want to miss me and kill your love or any of these helpless children around us now, do you?"

Tears streaked down Evelyn's face. "Jesse!"

"I know it's a little overly dramatic, but I figured what the hell. It's late, and this place is abandoned to begin with."

Evelyn shook her head frantically from side to side. She levelled her head. "Why?"

"It doesn't happen too often, but Tamara found out who I was so she had to be taken care of before she could disrupt my work."

Evelyn's bright blue eyes shifted from Jesse and back to Lily. "And just who are you?"

The emerald shimmered. "I'm the first woman ever created."

Evelyn was taken back. "You're Eve?"

Lily laughed. "That senseless berk. Hardly." She draped her right harm over Jesse's shoulder. "Eve was nothing more than a replacement. It was so easy to manipulate her to eat from that tree. Where do you think Milton came up with the idea to have Lucifer possess that serpent? The Bible?"

"If you're not Eve, then who are you?"

The emerald glistened. "Adam had a wife before her." She removed her arm from Jesse. "Her name was Lilith." She took a step closer to Evelyn. "I am she." She took another step forward.

"Don't come any closer!"

The emerald shimmered. "Sweetie, put down the pistol."

Evelyn took a step backwards. "Why the fuck should I do that?"

Her shaking finally caused a round to discharge from the magazine. It passed through the space in Lilith's chest just above where the pinstriped vest met the bustier. She did not flinch. The children began crying because of the noise.

Evelyn was dumbstruck. "You ... you should be dead."

Lilith paid no attention to the small wound in her chest as it was already starting to heal. "Honey, I've been run through with more weapons than days you've lived."

Evelyn's voice began to stumble. "You ... you can't be human ... it's not possible."

Lilith smiled with closed lips. "I assure you that I am. I'm the purest form of human being on this planet."

"No, you're trying to confuse me. You must be a daemon. No human can survive a wound like that."

Lilith laughed. "I am no daemon. Honestly, you people and your fanciful stories of succubi, lamias, and other creatures that have never existed. If everything in those tales were true, I would be birthing one hundred daemons a day so they could be killed just to fill the quota." She laughed again. "One hundred a day? That's ridiculous. I can't bear daemons. I'm human. I did meet those three angels whose names are written on amulets by superstitious parents though. Even though I don't cause sickness to infants, I should never have given them my word without knowing what it meant, but ..." She smirked. "I was young and rash."

"But even Adam and Eve died. If you're truly human, how have you lived for so long?"

"Simple. I never fell from grace."

Evelyn became puzzled.

"I left that garden before the whole Tree of Knowledge debacle. I am one of a select few who will never come to know death."

"There's more!"

Lilith nodded. "Only a few. My husband is one."

Evelyn had to inquire. "And is your husband unfallen, too? Is that how he will never come to know death?"

"Actually no."

"Then … who …" She took a few seconds to think. "Satan? Is that your fallen husband?"

Lilith chuckled. "First off, his name is Lucifer. Why can't you people get that through your heads? Satan is another being altogether. Second, why would I get myself involved with a celestial being? Fallen or not, he has no free will of his own. He's just an extension of Father's. Lucifer's expulsion from heaven was just Father having some self-doubts about his newest creations. When his conscious side won out, he tried to expel his doubt by banishing it to the pit." Lilith turned around and started making her way back to Jesse. "Then again, if Lucifer was Iblees, who is a Jinn and not an angel, then he did have his own free will, but even I don't know the full details of what goes on in different planes of existence. In any event, he is an enemy of man, as he wishes nothing more than destruction. We have no allegiance with him or his followers."

Evelyn's curiosity had gotten the better of her. "Who is your husband?"

"It's not rocket science. How could a man go off into the land of Nod, meet his wife, and father a tribe when the only woman around was back mourning for the death of her other son? Think back. Remember all those things you've forgotten over your years, fallen one. The things you pushed out of your mind because of your parents' fate."

Evelyn searched her memory for a moment until she thought she had the answer. "You mean Cain?"

Lilith grinned. "It was love at first sight. We became serpent and scythe and were charged with a mission." Lilith put her right palm on the center of her chest. The emerald blazed intensely. "The fun we had."

Evelyn did not understand. "But wait. Since Cain was born of fallen man, shouldn't he be dead? How is he able to still be breathing?"

"The mark protects him. He doesn't age, and he can't be killed. It was a blessing, not a curse. He was clever, tricking Father by stating the punishment was too much for him to bear. His cleverness did not end there though. As I told you on the first day we met, we both knew a day of reckoning was coming and his cleverness somehow secured our bloodline from being destroyed by that flood. Father was testing us, not them. I'm not sure if Cain realized that or not." She took a moment. "Though I'm unsure of how he secured our line, I can sense the blood of our lineage. I really wish I knew how he did it though. I'm willing to bet that he somehow brought out the potential of a son of Adam and used one of our own blood to carry the line. Until I meet him again, I won't truly know, but that does not change the fact that most, not all, of this world's populace has our blood in their veins."

Evelyn was still puzzled. "If that's the case, then why kill all these people, your children?"

She moved behind Jesse's chair. "I didn't kill anyone here. I rarely get my hands dirty. Just implant an idea into a person's head and sit back and enjoy the show. Look around." She placed out her right hand and moved it around the room in emphasis. "The marriage, the ups and downs you and Jesse have gone through these past months, and the lives of everyone around here. People are easy. The second I suggested to Bruce that his fellow partner was involved somehow, I knew he would kill everyone here. It wasn't my will to have these people die. Bruce could not have run amok. It was his decision."

"What about Father Bradley?"

"That was just a little fun on my part. I love to see what religious officials do when they find out the truth." She grinned. "The world can always use one less priest. I'm assuming that's what brought you here. You watched the news, and you remembered where you saw his face and then set the wheels in motion with Tamara and Seth."

"You knew that Jesse and I followed you that day?"

The emerald shone. "Of course I did."

"But what if I didn't catch the news?"

"I would have simply called your beeper from the phones at the reception desk or used a pain-filled sounding Jesse to call you at home. One way or another, you were going to show up here tonight."

"Why are you and your husband doing all this?"

Her anger did not faze Lilith's calm demeanour in any way. The emerald focused into Evelyn's widened, bright blue eyes. "The bloodline was strong in will and conviction once, but you people have diluted the stream with your mass repopulation and blood transfusions and whatnot. True will and conviction have been distorted with false definitions masked behind selfish reasons. You've become weak and easily corrupted. The gene pool keeps getting smaller and smaller, and our gift becomes weaker and weaker. Disease and medical conditions are rampant. A judgment day is coming. It may be self-inflicted or divinely brought, but, rest assured, it will come to pass sooner or later. We wish to make sure those bloodlines filled with strong will, faith, and conviction, regardless of creed or race, are the ones to have their influence survive into future generations. Maybe this time you won't dilute the stream to such an overwhelming degree."

Evelyn was shocked at Lilith's revelation. "All this is about blood and influence?"

She nodded her head. "Think of it for a moment. Blood is the very essence of life itself. Blood knows, sees, and remembers all. Blood is old. Blood is ancient. Blood is young. Blood knows of all the secrets hidden within the beings to which it inhabits. Blood is the only true driving force, coming from one originating source. Blood is eternal and makes all living creatures alike and immortal, even when death takes his toll. Many people do not deserve this power contained within. Its prestigious power can make even Father tremble, but we're not here to overthrow him. That's not our crusade."

"And what is your crusade?"

"Just think of us as liberators. You see, we have the potential to grow. We are not static in power as those celestial beings are."

"You make it sound as if you want warriors to wage a war on heaven."

Lilith placed her hands on Jesse's shoulders. "Now why would we want that? We have faith. Who needs religion when you have that? Religion starts wars, but faith settles the matter. Father may have his doubts. Whether he banishes them to the pit or not, they sometimes tend to resurface and creep their way into this world here. In a way, we do fight against Father as we battle with Lucifer and his followers. Even though all have not awakened yet, we have our warriors, and we sometimes join forces with the angels to drive back Lucifer and destroy his followers, whether they be human or celestial. We're perfecting what Father started so long ago. We're no different than a scientist who uses someone else's equation as a basis and expands on it."

Evelyn thought she knew where Lilith was headed. "So you're trying to create a new Eden?"

Lilith laughed quietly. "Harmony will never exist as long as Father has his doubts, and he always will."

Evelyn became frustrated. "Then why? Why all this trouble?"

"One cannot bay back Father's fallen side if one is not strong in conviction. We don't hold your hands and guide you through your life. When that happens, you people become soft and self-absorbed. You destroy the planet so you can place your new God in your wallets. You miss even the subtlest things and meanings and make mockeries of long-standing traditions and practices, such as faith, by inventing organized religions. You call all of this progress when it's all just another dark age to which Petrarch described. Only now, you have new toys."

"Why work with children then? Why not just kill us all and spare a few?"

"They're the most impressionable and susceptible to the positive traits of a strong will and conviction. A quick fix is no solution as it would not hold. The battle against corruption must start as soon as possible. When the darkness of this age has been dispersed, our descendants can come again in the former pure radiance."

Evelyn had nothing to say.

"As I said to you earlier, life is full of surprises."

Evelyn raised a brow.

"I came here to work solely on the premise of helping these children, but, as I spent more time around you, something happened that caught my attention and focused it toward you."

"What is that?"

"Your good physical health."

"My health?"

Lilith nodded her head up and down. "Normally, your health would not be enough to catch my eye, but, after I found out the weak stock that you came from, coupled with your character, views and what you've been through, it showed something strong and enduring inside of you."

"So you've been testing me?"

Lilith placed her arms around Jesse's neck and leaned forward so her head was next to his. "To be fair, I was testing you before I found out. This was also another reason why Tamara had to go."

She removed Bruce's pistol, which was hiding in between the backside of her pants and vest, with her right hand. She placed it on Jesse's temple. Jesse's screams were muffled as he closed his eyes. Evelyn cried out.

"Crying will get you nowhere here, Evelyn."

"You … you wouldn't kill him."

Lilith brought Bruce's pistol down and fired into Jesse's right thigh. Ryan's pistol fell from Evelyn's hands. It made a clanking noise that sounded quite odd as it was coupled by muffled screams, tears, and screaming children. Lilith brought Bruce's pistol back to Jesse's temple. Evelyn let out a yelling plea. "Don't hurt him!"

The emerald sparkled. "That depends on you, my dear. His life is in your hands."

"What?"

"Ticktock, Evelyn. Should I kill him or not?"

More tears began to streak down her cheeks as she reached her right hand out. "No!"

"Why not?" Lilith calmly inquired. "Because you love him?" Lilith turned her head slightly to look at Jesse. "With the way you two go at it and both of your doubts, that's not good enough a reason for me."

Evelyn looked forward in horror. Lilith turned her head back to Evelyn. "I'm going to count to five."

She had no idea what to say. Lilith started counting. The seconds passed like hours in the surge of everything that Evelyn had just heard and witnessed.

Lilith was about to call five when Evelyn yelled at her to stop.

She put the pistol to her right side and listened.

"There's nothing I can do to stop you."

The emerald gleamed forward with fascination.

"If I try to convince you of any reason why you shouldn't, it would just be a lie. If I tell you that I would do anything to save his life, then I submit my own will." She took in a deep breath. "I stand by whatever happens next, no matter how painful it may be to me. I have faith that all will work out in the long run."

The emerald pierced through Evelyn's bright blue eyes and into her soul. It scanned the fibre of her being and knew Evelyn was not lying. She placed the pistol back in between the backside of her pants and vest. The emerald became illuminated. "You're much smarter than your namesake was, Evelyn." She knelt down and began to untie Jesse. "Most people never catch that subtle double negative when I test them of will and faith." She removed his gag and backed away from the chair.

Jesse fell, and Evelyn rushed quickly over to the floor. Lilith was making her way to a basinet to calm a screaming child. She leaned forward and tucked the child under his blue covers, soothing his soul so he cried no longer. She made her way over to the doorway.

Evelyn turned her head. "Lilith!"

She turned around and faced Evelyn, whose arms were over Jesse as they were kneeling on the floor.

"You're just going to leave us here?" She took off her sweater and tied it around Jesse's leg as a tourniquet.

"I know how to make myself disappear. It will be as if I never worked here."

"Then what are we supposed to tell the police?"

Lilith smiled. "Well, it was Bruce's fault after all, wasn't it? I mean you were late coming into work, and Jesse came down here to visit with you during his break. He did not know that you were running behind schedule, but, when he did, he decided to wait for you in the nursery. When Bruce started to run amok, he tried to stop him from killing the children here in the nursery, and he was shot in his thigh from Bruce's pistol for his efforts. Bruce, delusional and crazed, thought he killed Jesse, as it was close range, when Jesse actually played dead after he hit the floor. Bruce didn't bother to check the body before walking out of the nursery, where he took his own life. You showed up shortly after this transpired and decided to take Ryan's pistol for self-defence after you saw the bodies. You made your way to the nursery to check on the children, and you found Jesse laying there with blood flowing out of his thigh. You ran over to him. After you asked him what happened, he told you the whole story."

The couple looked forward at her.

"At least that's the way it appears to look, right? Although the chair seems as if it should belong in the reception area." Lilith smirked and turned around. She took a couple of steps forward before turning around again. "I almost forgot."

She took something out of her pants pocket. She threw it toward them. It landed on the floor in front of them and slid the rest of the way. Evelyn picked it up. It was a set of keys. Jesse and Evelyn looked hard at it.

"I already transferred the ownership to your names. All of my possessions are out of the house so you'll have to furnish it for yourselves. If anyone asks," she said slyly, "you can tell them it was a wedding gift from a long-lost relative."

They looked up at her.

"Weather the storm, you two, and make sure you have children. They will greatly benefit the world if you guide them in proper will and conviction."

Lilith left the nursery for the final time. She began walking toward the stairwell with the rope and gag used to restrain Jesse in her left hand. She stopped in front of Bruce and knelt over to place his pistol back in its holster, but did not snap the strap back into place. She left the body and reached the stairwell door. She placed her right hand on the handle and pressed her thumb down on the lock lever, leaving Evelyn and Jesse to their own devices. Lilith had much work ahead of her, especially as she was about to begin her stay as a professor of humanities at Kingsford Shire Coeducational Boarding School.